ONE

SOLDIER'S

MINUTE

TERESA M. SHAFER

ONE SOLDIER'S MINUTE

TERESA M. SHAFER

woodhall press

Woodhall Press | Norwalk, CT

woodhall press

Woodhall Press, 81 Old Saugatuck Road, Norwalk, CT 06855
WoodhallPress.com

Cover design: Asha Hossain
Layout artist: L.J. Mucci

Library of Congress Cataloging-in-Publication Data available

ISBN 978-1-954907-86-7 (paper: alk paper)
ISBN 978-1-954907-87-4 (electronic)

First Edition
Distributed by Independent Publishers Group
(800) 888-4741

Printed in the United States of America

This is a work of fiction. Names, characters, businesses, events
and incidents are the products of the author's imagination. Any
resemblance to actual persons, living or dead, or actual events is
purely coincidental.

Dedicated to my father, Steven H. Shafer, who fought in World War II, and my brother Edward E. Shafer who is a Vietnam Veteran. Also, to all my ancestors who fought in the Revolutionary War, the Civil War, the Mexican Border War, and World War, I and to all Combat Veterans, thank you for doing what others only dream of doing, for being the brave and strong warriors who help to keep this country safe and free. We owe you more than can ever be repaid.

FOREWORD

As you pick up this book and read my character's life, I would like you to have these words in your mind so that you may reach a richer understanding.

A friend of mine confided in me that she had family members who had been in combat but who had chosen not to speak to her about it and this, although she did not say, clearly made her feel slighted or untrusted.

To her I had this answer:

"Do you know why they do not want to talk to you about it? I can tell you if you really want to know.

They feel embarrassed about what they have done, and they feel guilty as well. They have done some horrific things, and, in the end, they see you and are embarrassed because they are afraid that you won't understand them. That you, a person who they love and respect will not understand why they did the things they did. So, they stay silent. They don't want to tell you because if they do, and you learn what they have done, you may not love them anymore. They can bear the weight of what they have done, as long as you love them. But if they tell you, then maybe you won't love them and that is a weight that they cannot bear."

To the combat veterans out there reading this missive, please understand that in telling your stories to those you love, it will not change how much they love you. It might change how they see you. But I promise you, they will see you in a stronger, more sympathetic light, not to pity you, God forbid, but to understand you and to help you if you want help.

All of us need help from time to time and there is no greater help than that which comes from a loved one. Those who know you best, are the ones to ask for help. It is safe to tell them your stories, help them to understand why you did what you did, and let their love heal your heart.

Please, before you pick up that bottle of alcohol or pills, hear me, you do not need to drown out the pain. You need to release it and conquer your fear. Tell someone. Help them to understand, and then work your way out of the rabbit hole that you have lost yourself in, with their help.

With respect,
Teresa

1

The Party

I blink a snowflake from my eye. Nothing has changed down-range. The long stretch of road that I had been staring down was still empty and silent before me. I am in northern Afghanistan. It is late December, and the air is a crisp 28 degrees. It is too cold to truly snow, and the cold has turned the snow that had already fallen into hard unforgiving ice crystals that make far too much noise when you move and leaves obvious tracks. It had not been easy mucking into this hole while covering my footfalls and trying but failing miserably at being quiet. Knowing that I would wake the dead with my passage, I chose to move as quickly as possible. When I found this nice little nest of scrub, the scarf that was wrapped around my face and my eyelashes were covered in ice from my breath and my lungs were burning. Still, my spotter and I wasted no time settling in for the long haul. I had a nice winter camo waterproof blanket to lay on and I was covered with another one. We were both in the same winter scrub pattern clothing and even my girl Mary that is my rifle, was dressed in brown and white.

Within a few hours of arrival, the wind had picked up and buried us and our tracks in drifted snow. There isn't much in the way of vegetation to stop the snow from drifting. Northern Afghanistan is a high desert, so they don't get a lot of water to support much. The ground supports low scrub bushes, cheat-grass, and some smaller trees like Manzanita and Hawthorn with the occasional pine tree trying to make a life out of the rocks. Mostly those are stunted and growing at an angle away from the driving wind.

The berm that I had perched on had most likely been the reason that the desolate road I was watching made the near 90-degree turn in front of me. It was the perfect spot for a sniper like me to stare directly into the passenger compartment of any oncoming car. For a guy like the idiot I was here to eliminate to take such a road was pure arrogance. His loss, my gain.

My spotter and I have settled into an uneven cadence. Uneven, because even and predictable can be spotted and attributed to human behavior, whereas uneven breathing and movement are more animal-like and less likely attributed to a human. Sometimes, you should take the time to watch a bird or a cat or any animal really, none of them move like humans.

As I wait, my thoughts drift.

—————

My mind is filled with an altogether different scene in which the world was covered in quiet, peaceful snow. My wife Patricia and our children, Michael and Bella, clinging desperately together while Patti tried to teach them how to ice skate. I was supposed to be helping. Instead, I stood near the bushes by

2

the frozen lake and watched the antics of my family and the dire predicament of my beloved. I love watching Patti with the children. She is so patient and smiles all the time. She so clearly loves them, and it glows in her eyes. It reminds me of my own mother and how she used to look at me and Katie, my sister. A snowflake drifts into view, in my memory or reality, it does not matter, the image fades and my cadence continues.

I exhale. Slowly. Deliberately, so the vapor of my breath is not seen. The vapor hisses silently between my teeth and drifts up toward my eyes. A nearly imperceptible puff of wind pulls the vapor away and eradicates its existence. I allow the pause between my exhale and my next breath to stretch.

I do not know how long we will wait for our target. But my mind can fill the minutes.

My wife, Patti, was an amazing find. The first time I saw her, my heart nearly exploded in my chest. She was perfect in every way. I had to speak to her. I had to have her as my own, forever. How could I not want her? I was entranced by the way that her black hair bounced on her shoulders when she walked and how it framed her perfect face. That face, that perfect face illuminated by two perfect dancing green eyes and that soft, oh-so-touchable skin the color of coffee with a double dollop of cream and that tiny dimple on her chin. I walked right up to her and introduced myself. It was magic from that moment on. Of course, that is the story I tell myself. It is not what happened.

The first part is true. Patti is utterly amazing in every way, and my heart did nearly explode, or at least it felt that way.

3

After that part, however, it is a total fabrication. I did walk up to her, with about a dozen other men and me, Steven Washington Harrington the class clown, the non stop talker, was tongue-tied. My buddy, Doug, got the first dance and every dance and moment after.

Patti is the only person in the world who I have trouble talking to, even now. Back then it was worse. It is not that she intimidates me or makes me feel inadequate, no, she entrances me. How does one speak to a dream? She is everything and all things and I am simply stunned to have the opportunity, no, the *right* to speak to her. I do not know what it was I felt when I looked at her, was that what love felt like? I was simply paralyzed with awe. I suppose, had I been given enough time, I would have stuttered out something akin to speaking, but Doug was like lightning, and I was molasses.

According to my other friends, I was seriously thinking of deleting Doug from my list of friends. They also told me that I had looked like a lost puppy for the remainder of the party. I am sorry, did I not mention that we were at a party? It was a Unit Christmas party. Generally speaking, Unit Christmas Parties are the place where people get inebriated, and all manner of shenanigans and Tom foolery happen. In truth, any kind of party or even a get-together that involves military personnel results in chaos, followed by practical jokes and mass amounts of vomiting and chronic memory loss. This is allowed to happen most especially when these military men and women will soon be deploying and when they return from a successful mission. The opportunity to let off steam and relax does not happen that often when you are deployed, and when you are on mission, your head needs to be screwed on straight, because although we all accept that we may die doing whatever it is we are doing, we would rather not. But that ghost of the possibility is always lingering in our minds.

Anyway, Patti was not in the military, she was a military brat. She was the daughter of one of the generals who had come to base to oversee our training. The General had met her mother, a woman who was and is extremely well put together, and incidentally passed those attributes on to her daughter, while he was stationed in California. Esperanza Isabella Gonzales was in the United States on a work visa and had a job working on her uncle's food truck. Her Uncle Felix had a contract with the base to sell in the parking lot from 1130 hours until 1330 hours. This is where butter-bar Lieutenant Michael Grant Erickson, a man who was obviously of Viking descent, met his pretty little Senorita Esperanza.

They dated for the better part of two-years before tying the knot. They had four children, two of each. Their eldest, a boy they had named Alfonso Michael, was killed in a convenience store one afternoon where he and two of his school friends had stopped on their way home from soccer practice. He was mistaken by the clerk, a man of Middle Eastern descent, to be a gangbanger. Alfonso was shot dead at the scene, one of his friends spent weeks in the hospital with a bullet in his head and is still in therapy while the third boy escaped any serious physical injury, but has, since it happened, increasingly been involved with the community to educate the community in gang violence awareness. This incident made fourteen-year-old Patricia the eldest with Maribelle and Jimmy rounding out the family. It also caused the freshly minted light Colonel Erickson to move his family to the Midwest.

As it turned out, it had been Patti who had gotten mixed up in the gangs. She had been just as pretty as a girl as she was as a woman, and the leader of one of the smaller gangs had taken an interest. After sweet talking her into thinking he wasn't such a bad guy and convincing her that her parents were just too strict and didn't understand the real world, he took her to his bed and really messed her up. She had been twelve years old. She doesn't talk about it much even today, and when she does, she falls short of saying whether her participation had been entirely voluntary, if you know what I mean.

Her parents watched their little girl become withdrawn, angry, and evasive. It was a far cry from the outgoing star of the show that she had been. But, when Alfonso died, things changed in the Erickson household. The children were confined to the base and when they went out, one of their parents was always with them. Then they moved and in time their little girl rebounded. There will always be a scar, but Patti was able to relegate that time of her life to a manageable place in her mind.

So... We were in Texas being spun up for some kind of big shindig that was all but completely top secret. This was not our home base. The Christmas Party only happened because we were waiting on rounds and equipment. Well, to be fair, it would have happened without us, even had our crap not been in the wind. So, we were in the right place at the right time, and we would soon be out and once we were actually deployed in country to complete that mission, we probably would not see stateside again for at least a year. The party was a very welcome impromptu send off.

It would have been welcome, except that I spent the entire party in the corner, drinking myself into a coma and trying not to glare at Doug and Patti. I wanted her, dammit! Unfortunately, this was not my moment, or our moment. It was theirs.

We deployed to the sandbox ten days later. Wait... Why do we call it the sandbox you ask? Well, first off, it is the sand box because to actually tell people, like your loved ones, which country you are going to for a mission, can be dangerous. You know that "loose lips sink ships" and breaking Op Sec, that's operational security, can get your son or daughter killed. So, stop asking them where they are going. If they are not telling you, they are just trying to keep everyone safe. So, just wish them well and welcome them home when they get back. And second off, I bet you thought that I forgot the second reason, all of those countries have a lot of sand. Just sand. Everywhere.

Our gear and rounds arrived four days after we did. The mission was more important than the gear. We had a job to do. The four days actually gave us some time to get our sit rep, that means that we needed to find out what we were doing and what the enemy was doing and acclimate to the new environment.

The locals both loved us and at the same time, some of them hated us. It was a real pain in the ass figuring out which ones were which. Something that most people do not understand about the people who live in the sand box, there are lots of different tribes and nations represented in a single city in any given country, or even just an area. Not all of them are friendly towards outsiders, especially Americans.

The local version of military is very confusing. When we are in country, we share a base with any number of different factions. Every tribe or nation has their own version of military and some of them are little more than thugs wearing mismatched uniforms, and some are worse. The one thing that they all have in common is that they all want something from the Americans. Almost all of them want to have some kind of dick measuring contest with us, in any manner, even if it's just winning at dice. Oddly enough, not all of them are looking to bed our women, many come from countries where women are for breeding and men are for fun. You've really got to be careful of those guys, especially in the shower! They bring a whole new meaning to the term "buddy shower."

All of the veiled and not so veiled hostility towards Americans causes us to become a stronger team. Because, if you are not part of the team, then you are out in the cold and sometimes the cold hides some nasty predators. All the petty boot camp shit goes out the window and people either learn to get along or they get left in the cold.

On the flip side of this, are the actual civilians in the area. They are generally well disposed towards Americans because the presence of Americans means that there will be food, and water and all manner of new things to be given or traded. Now when I say civilian, I mean people that are not in the local military or militia or any kind of other military-style group. Sometimes that line gets really blurry. Right now, I am talking about normal everyday people who farm the land, wash clothing, and do all of the things that no one else wants to do. Those people, generally, love Americans. Unfortunately, you cannot count on them for anything, except trying to sell you something while you are fighting for your life and they will never choose you over the local government because let's face it, they've got to live there when we go home to baseball and donuts. Going back to "life" after the Americans bug out can get super dicey for those who helped us, even those that simply interpreted for us. If you do not believe me, ask anyone who was our ally in Afghanistan, wait, you can't. We left them behind to face whatever. Now the world knows why Americans are not everyone's favorite people.

When the mission is over, is it tough to walk away when you see something that pulls at your heartstrings, yeah, it is, but getting personally involved only works in Hollywood. In the real world, people get hurt and die and American involvement generally doesn't end well for anyone involved, because, no you can't just put a family of locals onto the plane or chopper and if you try to help them and fail, then the local tyrant will be more than happy to eradicate them and everyone and everything they know and love in the most painful and humiliating way possible. And for your trouble, when you get home, if you are lucky, you might get demoted and moved to a janitor job. More than likely, you will get a DHD, that's a dishonorable discharge, and no it is not good. You would have been better off spending time in Leavenworth prison, and in case you were wondering, yes you can get time in military prison, only to get a DHD when you get out. It all depends on how much your actions embarrassed the United States and how much political damage you caused. Real people do not get medals for saving a wayward doctor and a hundred villagers. They get medals for doing their jobs as they are designed and completing the objective without causing an international incident.

Anyway.... When our crap arrived, we loaded up a land transport and headed out. Only the lieutenant knew where we were headed. We just headed down a dirt road that led to nowhere. After an hour of driving, you could see only desert in a 360. I was glad that he knew where we were going, most of us had no idea where we had been. It was the sand box, that was the sum total of what we knew. When we got to where we were going, we would be told all that we needed to know. Who cares what country we were in? I sure didn't. We were not here to affect politics or mix with the locals for posterity. We were a sniper unit. When we got sent somewhere, we were there for only one reason, to kill someone, or several someone's, and get out without causing an uproar.

It is easier this way. I think so, anyway. I have no attachments, to people or places. I go in, do my job, and go on to the next job, until I am rotated out for some time stateside. Right now, I am sitting on a small berm, in a cold country waiting for my target to show himself. The road is long, and it has a few turns, but when his car is finally in site, he will be headed straight into my sites for nearly a mile. That is plenty of time for me to do my job.

I admit, after I married Patti, this lifestyle did become a bit tedious. I still do not care where I am, but I do not like the long tours overseas. My friends tell me that I am getting old. They may be right. Retirement is right around the corner. I have been in now for nearly twenty-five years and I joined when I was eighteen. That makes me a whopping forty-two years old. Sometimes I feel like I am eighty. But I am still young, and I have plans for the rest of my life. Eighteen months and I am out, six months and I am in sanctuary. So, six months to go, before I am home for good. This shot, the one that I am lined up on right now, will be my last. It has more meaning in many respects than my first shot. That one, well that one changed my life in a not so positive way.

Let me tell you something about soldiering and shooting someone, from my point of view. Setting up and working on your fundamentals and then firing on a paper or even a metal target, well they're just targets, aren't they? They don't turn into red mist when the round hits them or ooze buckets of blood on the sand. A paper target just marks the passage of a round by leaving a nice neat little hole in the paper. If you are good, all the little holes will be in a nice tight little pattern, if you are really good you will overlap holes and have rounds go through the same holes. But shooting a target of any kind is not like shooting a human being.

The first time that you squeeze the trigger and take a person's life—now that is an experience that I do not wish on anyone. That is an odd thing for a sniper to say. I just told you that I am very okay with my job and I am not overly concerned about what others do for their jobs, that being said, killing a person for no reason that you can fathom, that act changes a person on a personal level, and not usually in a positive way. So yes, I would rather folks that have sentimentality about killing another person just not pick up a gun or put themselves in that situation.

My first time was as a foot soldier. My squad and I were on patrol on the outskirts of a largish city in some sandbox county. We were outside the wire. I was the rookie in the squad. I had deployed once before and seen no action. Then I was moved to a different squad for this deployment as a substitute for a guy who dropped out at the last minute. We had been fighting insurgents for months. Just when we thought that we had eradicated the nest, more would swarm seemingly out of the sand. Our job was to defend this city and its civilian inhabitants. I am fairly certain that at least half the folks in the city did not care one way or the other if we protected them, in fact, I am pretty certain that some of the folks in the city were the insurgents that we fought. And to be clear, yes, I fired a lot of rounds at shadows and into doorways and windows. I probably hit someone, but I never actually investigated. Generally, there was never any time for random investigation inside the city.

Anyway, we were on patrol on the outskirts to the north and in the north were some low mounds of hard-baked sand with some rocks and boulders thrown about in a rough jumble. It was a good place for a small group of people to hide. We knew this, so we were keeping a close eye on the area when as the sun was on its last legs peaking over the horizon to our left, five or six dusty people appeared in that pile of rocks and sand. Each was holding something long and gun-shaped in their hands.

I don't know who fired first. All I remember was the sound of a lot of guns firing at the same time and me dropping to the ground trying to find some concealment behind a scruffy-looking bush while getting off a few rounds with my own rifle in the general direction of the rocks.

Having successfully rolled behind that small bush where I was harder to see and thus harder to shoot, I surveyed the scene through the branches. It was really just a quick look while I was setting myself up to take some kind of aim at an actual target from my prone position. It took about two seconds, which when you are being shot at, is a long time to not be shooting back. I spotted some guy wrapped in dirty white native clothing. His rifle was bucking regularly as he fired it from the hip. He wasn't aiming, he was just spraying bullets at a location off to my left. I dropped my eye to the site on my standard issue M-16 rifle, flicked the safety to Burst and squeezed the trigger, just like I had been taught. My rifle (I had named that one Martha) gave a quick buck into my shoulder and my vision slowed. You all have had that experience at least once in your life, where time seems to move slowly, and you can see everything happen. Well, the second that I squeezed off those rounds I felt like I could see them travel through the air and then I saw them hit that guy. He was at a slight angle to me, so the rounds, three of them, struck him on the left side of his chest. They pushed him back a little and lifted him slightly off the ground. His body folded around the entry points, which were in a tight group just above his left pectoral nipple, and he crumbled to the ground like a discarded rag doll. Once he was on the ground, time started again. Most of the shooting had stopped. I could still hear at least one M-16 barking and a scattering of the MP-5's that the insurgents were using. But those sounds seemed to be moving away from us.

12

The next sound that I heard was my squad leader ordering us to advance. So, I climbed off of the ground. My legs were shaking, and I thought I might fall. I didn't want to embarrass myself. This wasn't my squad. I didn't know how they would react if I fell over. I took a deep breath and willed my legs to move like normal. I fell back on my training and moved forward with the other guys, toward the rocks.

When we came upon the first body, I puked in my mouth a little. But again, I willed my body to obey. This guy looked like he had been shredded and stuffed into a bag. Everything, every part of his body had a hole in it and blood was everywhere. I had never even seen this one. When we had hit the ground, I had rolled away from the squad and my view had been obscured by the wave of the sand and these damn rocks.

Blood soaks into sand the same way that water does, it leaves a slightly darker stain, but that is all. The sand drinks it all and within minutes, were it not for the body, a person might not know that a man had died here. We continued. We moved slowly, expecting another ambush. We peeked around and over every rock, muzzle first. We found blood spattered on lots of rocks and wet spots in the sand where someone had either bled or urinated. Sometimes, the smell told us which. Urine that comes from fear, smells like fear.

Finally, we did come upon the man I had shot. From where the rest of my squad had hunkered down, they would not have been able to see him. He was just as I remembered him. Folded in on his wounds and lying in a sandy wet spot on his right side. His head tilted awkwardly toward the sun, his hand still clutching the Russian made MP-5. Puke rose into my throat once again. My knees wanted to buckle and all I could think was, "Who is going to miss this man tonight? His wife, his children... his mother?" But as I was falling down that rabbit

13

hole, my squad leader, a big blond Norwegian-looking man by the name of Roberson walked into my vision and bent over the body. I heard the body shift slightly while at the same time I heard a light snap, like a string breaking. Roberson turned around to face me. His hand extended towards me with a charm dangling on a string hanging from his fingers. He had a wide grin on his face. "Congratulations, Rookie. You bagged yourself your first sand nigger for a birthday present!" Roberson was a serious ass. He wasn't even a good squad leader. But he was what I had at the time. Rumor had it that when he got home, he was asked to retire early. I don't really know what the circumstances were. Like I said, it wasn't my squad, they weren't even from the same State of the Union.

Go ahead and ask, did I take the charm? Of course, I took the charm! Not because I wanted it, but because if I hadn't, I would have looked weak and may have died from friendly fire, and none of you would have ever heard my story. And yes, I took the charm and I tucked it away and every time I look at it, or just think about it, I pray for that man's family. It isn't much, some may think that it isn't enough, but it is all I can do.

I had forgotten that my birthday had been the week before and this was a bleak reminder that I had just turned 19. That charm on a string is tucked into a small chest that I keep in the back of my bottom drawer. My mom's rosary and my parent's wedding rings are in there too, along with a pile of letters and a bloody lock of my sister's hair. I see all their faces and more, every time I close my eyes. I do not sleep much.

Another snowflake drifts into my view. Several more join it. Great, it is beginning to snow. It must have warmed up a bit. I came prepared for this. My glass is covered.

Suddenly, my leg twitches involuntarily. It is infinitesimal, but I felt it and heard a slight shift in the blanket beneath me. A place on my leg is on fire. It needs to be itched. I ignore it. It will go away on its own, eventually.

2

My Personal History

Maybe, I should tell you all a little about me before I go on about my life in the Army. How did I get into the Army, you ask? Well, a lot of people join the military for a lot of different reasons. Some join so the military will pay for their schooling, some join because they have an itch that they cannot scratch and some, like me, join because they believe in the mission. Which mission is that? That is the mission of protect, defend, and fight. I wanted to be the wall that protects, the stone that defends and the hammer that fights, but I did not start out that way.

My mother and father were upper middle-class people. Mom stayed at home to raise me and my sister, Katie. She was really good at making jams, jellies, pie fillings and canning in general. She had her own little side business and used the profits to fund our extra-curricular activities. Things like sports, drama club, Girl Scouts, and the like. I think that she also used the money to buy us those "one special gifts" at Christmas, but I don't really know for sure. It just seems like something Momma would do.

Daddy was an auto mechanic. He was the finest man that I have ever known or ever will know. While Momma was the one who held our hands and wiped our brows when we were sick, daddy was the one who was the rock where we could all place our anchor. He was the leg that we stood behind when we were toddlers and the man I still try to make proud.

Growing up, my sister and I were thick as thieves. We would pull pranks on Mom all the time. Like hiding her jam strainer and blaming it on the dog, then putting it back while she searched the house. Things like that led to Mom finding things for us to do that were less annoying to her. We had one of those sets of encyclopedias that weigh a ton and take up two full shelves on a large bookcase. One day, after one of our pranks, Mom challenged us to "find something interesting" in one of those big heavy books and then tell her about it and she would judge who had found the most interesting bit of knowledge and give the winner a cookie hot from the oven. Well, that was a challenge that Katie and I could get behind.

Our first offerings were very sparse. We had not taken the time to really read what the topic was about, so we both failed. But Momma never said that we failed. She just asked us a hundred questions about the topic that we could not answer. Then she sent us back to find out more information because she didn't have time to stop and read, she needed us to tell her about our topic. That first time was all about learning how Momma would judge our efforts, every day after that it was about outperforming each other. On the days she baked, we knew that an encyclopedia contest was on the menu. Mom would help us sometimes by saying things like, "Gee, wouldn't it be nice if this section had a picture so we could see what they are describing?" Katie and I began drawing pictures to use as props as we explained our topic. If our topic was about a country, Mom would ask, "I wonder, how does all of this affect the countries around it." We would go back in and read about every country that bordered the one that we were presenting. Needless to say, we absorbed a huge percentage of those Encyclopedias before we ever started school, but even after going to school, we didn't stop the contests. They just took a backseat to homework. Mom did her part to motivate us, but at the same time she realized a cookie for our efforts would not yield positive results in the end. Hence, mom curbed us away from the cookies and began to sit down with us to share an apple or two while Katie and I presented what we had found in those oversized books.

When I started school, we had to have our contests on the weekends, because on the weekdays Momma would help me with my homework and Katie would try to draw on it. It was in first grade when I realized I knew a lot more than the other kids in my class. There was no topic that the teacher could bring up that I had not read something about in one of those books. That did not make me very popular with the other kids, because I instantly became the teacher's pet. I didn't know the teacher's pet was something to be avoided. I just wanted to share what I knew, because Katie and I had so much fun learning this stuff together I thought my new classmates would have fun too. Boy was I wrong. I made sure to tell Katie about all of this so that when she came to school, she wouldn't make the same mistake.

As we grew older, Katie naturally gravitated towards Mom and me, towards Dad. He taught me how to change the oil on our car when I was 10. What he didn't tell me during that little venture was to not put my head directly under the drain plug. Yup, you guessed it, I got completely doused with black

19

dirty oil. I thought my dad was going to split his gut laughing. Mom, on the other hand, did not find it amusing at all. She grabbed the bottle of Ivory dish soap, cuz Dawn had not yet been invented for public use and I sat in the bathtub in hot water, in more ways than one, until she could coax at least 70% of the oil out of my hair. Then we had to scrub my entire body because the water had gone cold, and the oil had stuck to my skin... and the tub. Mom was not happy. Daddy had to go out and get Mom some flowers the next day.

At church on Sunday that same week, I overheard Momma talking to one of her church friends about the incident with the oil. She spoke as if she were still angry, but her eyes danced with laughter and when she was done with the story, both she and her friend laughed and called Daddy incorrigible. I had to look that up when I got home and they called me silly, that word I knew.

We were a normal family, living in an ordinary city doing what every other American family does and believing what every other American family believes. At least that's what Katie and I both believed to be true. Going to school and interacting with others both our age and older showed us a whole new world. For example, not everyone's daddy was still at home. I still do not understand how kids can grow up proper without a father? And how can mommas be both soft and comforting and strong as a rock? I understand that part now, but back then, it was a mystery. I still believe that kids without good fathers, or good mothers for that matter, are really missing out on something beautiful. But they aren't given a choice, are they?

Still, Katie and I grew up in a Norman Rockwell picture. We had two caring parents, a stay-at-home mom, and a loving sibling... oh and don't forget Dusty our fluffy Golden Retriever who loved to roll in the dirt and "dust" the house, much to

Mom's chagrin. That is how he got his name. The second time that he did that, Mom called him that "dusty damn dog" and told us to get him out of the house until we could dust him off. Hence, the name Hunter was canned, and the dog became Dusty.

The older we got, the more Daddy and Momma would tell us stories about their own childhoods and their lives in general. Apparently, Daddy had fought in World War II and Momma had been a nurse during the conflict. Daddy didn't tell any bloody war stories, he only told funny ones. Now days looking back on those times, I understand why Daddy only told the funny stories. That meant that he had actually been in the shit. Because people who have been in the shit during a conflict seldom, if ever, talk about that stuff with their civilian family.

Daddy told us stories about life on a Navy ship during the war in the Pacific. Yeah, Daddy was a Navy man. He never told me what ship he was on. He talked about being on a small boat called a PT boat and them having the job of running decoy for Admiral Nimitz and the American fleet. But a PT boat in the Pacific had to have a port of call, someplace to dock, refuel and resupply, because there is a lot of water between islands out there. Personally, I think sometimes the bigger transport ships that carted the Marines around with their landing craft, also had a PT boat or two in their bellies. What better place to hide a little fish than inside a bigger fish? But that's just speculation and oddly enough, there are still a lot of secrets that the military is not telling concerning WWII. So, it cannot be verified.

Anyway, Daddy's Captain would have the crew send out false radio signals to lure the Japanese fleet away from the American fleet. When Daddy told this story, he would smile and say, "When they bit, we would lead them on a merry chase...

21

and pray like hell that our boat didn't break down." Which it apparently did on more than one occasion. One was while he and his crew mates were having a beer while parked in the bay of Japan and watching the Allies bomb the Mitsubishi factory. "Now the bay, you see, was peppered with mines," he would say in a conspiratorial tone. "We slipped in dodging those things while the planes dropped their bombs. No one was paying any attention to our little boat in the harbor." He would take a drag from his cigarette and clear his throat. "So, there we were in the bay in our skivvies drinking beer and watching the fireworks, when the Comm guy came up on deck and told us that the Japs were coming with their fleet." Daddy would always chuckle at this point in the story. "Well, we all jumped up, way too fast and a few of the boys got the heaves. Then it was assholes to elbows and bare feet slapping the metal deck as we all ran to our posts. Now our crew got to the engine room, expecting the engine to be purring away. But it wasn't. That was a bit of a shock and not just a little concerning. It took a minute for all of us, in our slightly drunken state to realize that the Skipper was hitting the right buttons, but the boat was not starting." He would stop to chuckle again and take another drag, while drawing out the suspense of the story. "It didn't take long to grasp that the armature that runs the electrical on the ship was broken. Nothing was going to start without a new one. Lucky for us, we had one in the bow of the ship... under fifty cases of beer and about a thousand pounds worth of other replacement parts." Another chuckle and drag and he continued. "Well, you ain't never seen half drunken men sober up so damn fast or move with such purpose. We had to get that 2000-pound armature from one end of the boat, to the other, hook it up and crank it, before the Japanese fleet boxed us into the harbor." Half the time he would stop his story here and someone would have to ask a question to coax the ending out of him. The other half of the time he would just shake his head and wrap it up with this, "Well, needless to say, I am here so we managed to get the damn thing hooked up alright and get out of there, but we could see their lights and hear their engines while we slipped out of the bay." He would smile lightly at the memory, take another drag off of his cigarette and say quietly, "Still, it was the best damn fireworks display that any of us have ever seen." Of course, it wasn't a fireworks display, it was bombs exploding which set off thousands of gallons of aircraft fuel. It was the sounds of detonations, metal twisting, glass exploding and people screaming in pain or fear and dying in both. But that is not what Daddy would tell us. He told the adventurous and funny story and left it at that.

Some of the other stories that he would tell us, now that I think of it, were much darker. He told us about how he got into the Navy to begin with. During the draft, everyone of age had to report to the high school. There in the gym were three officers, one for each branch. Daddy watched the men at the front of the line and as he drew closer to his turn to stand before the officers, he noticed that most of the guys were getting foot sol dier, because the Army officer kept reaching over and slamming his giant stamp onto nearly everyone's induction papers. What the draftee wanted was not making any difference whatsoever. If they asked for the Navy, the Army guy would just slam the stamp down. Occasionally, the Marine would stamp one, but that was usually on the big corn-fed farm boys. Daddy was not a big man, and he did not want to be in the infantry. When it was his turn, he stepped up as tall as he could before those men and when they asked him which branch of the military he wanted to be in he said, "Well sir, I don't much care, but I'm pretty sure that I would get seasick if you put me on one of

23

those big boats." And that is when the admiral said, "Boy, I am going to teach you not to call my ships a big boat!" and "slam" the admiral stamped Daddy's card. Daddy couldn't help it. He smiled so big that the admiral knew that he had been tricked.

After everyone got their laugh on and congratulated daddy for outsmarting the drafting process, daddy would tell us a story or two about how he and his brother Calvin would play tricks on their skippers while in port. He and Uncle Calvin looked like twins even though Daddy was two years younger. Sometimes they would swap ships and show up in roll call pretending to be each other. At first the bosman's mate would catch the switch and sometimes not. They found it to be great fun to see if anyone would notice that "Calvin" was not Calvin, but Steve, yes, I was named after my father. They stopped this little ruse after Daddy got caught up in an inspection and had no idea what his brother's actual job on the boat was and nearly got the entire boat disqualified or as they say it, "not seaworthy." WWII, after all was very serious business and although there was time for high jinks and laughter, there was a time and place for such things and during an inspection from the Fleet Admiral's Office was not the right time or place.

Daddy liked talking about his brother Calvin. They had been close as children and young men, but Calvin had not come home from the war. I think now that part of Daddy had died with his brother and part of his brother remained alive in my Daddy.

Sometimes, Daddy would tell the story of how he became a scout and raider. He would tell us that after his ship had crossed into the Pacific and after it had delivered men and supplies to Hawaii an old Navy captain had boarded the ship. He asked for volunteers to take part in a new program. Then he picked the people he wanted; most had not raised their hands. Daddy never said if he had or not. Those men were taken from the ship and put onto a boat, not a PT boat, but a larger one. Then they were taken out into the Pacific and after some travel, they parked a mile or so off the coast of a small island. Each man was stripped down to his skivvies and handed a knife. They were told that the island was infested with Japs and that Admiral Nimitz needed the island cleared of hostiles, but no one was to know that the Navy had ever been there. So, in the dark of night the men were told to swim to shore, kill all the Japs and return to the boat. Those that returned were on the team, those that didn't... well they wouldn't be on the team. Obviously, Daddy came back, but his swimming skills were not what you would call Olympic quality. But all teams need to have technical people to help them do their jobs, so instead of being one of the men that did island incursions, he was an electrician on a PT boat so that other men could swim to the islands, and he helped his PT boat run decoy for the American fleet.

Momma was a lot less complicated. She had been raised on a farm. When the war came, she went out and learned how to be a nurse. Unfortunately for her, the sight of blood made her stomach turn, so she usually emptied bed pans, changed linen, and did all the jobs that one does when one works in a hospital and pukes at the sight of blood. Still, she contributed to the war effort like every other warm-blooded American and I am proud to be her child.

So, I bet y'all are wondering how the heck my parents could have been involved in the world war. Well, they were older parents, that is to say that Momma was past her childbearing years when she and Daddy got together, but they loved each other so much that God blessed them, twice. I always knew, well I assumed anyway, that my parents would leave us while Katie and I were still fairly young. They might see a grandchild or two before passing, but they would not be there in our middle years. What I did not see coming is what actually happened.

It was just another day. I was 15, Katie was 13. We had gone out to dinner. Nothing fancy, just a nice meal as a family. On the way home, we were in a left turn lane to get onto the freeway, and it happened. Katie and I were teasing each other about something that I do not remember when the car jerked forward. I remember glass breaking and pebbles of it flying past my turned face, as I had been looking to my left at my sister. Then, I remember my head hitting something and then I woke up in the hospital. My Aunt Shirley was there, Mom's sister. My head hurt. Aunt Shirley called the nurse. They put me back to sleep.

When I woke up again, days had passed, at least that is what they told me. They had induced a coma so that my head could heal. There had been a lot of swelling. I asked where my parents were, where Katie was. Aunt Shirley told me that my mother was in a different room. She was still in a coma, not chemically induced. I didn't know what that meant. Is there a difference? Of course, there is, but I was a boy. I didn't know at the time. Aunt Shirley wouldn't tell me about my father or sister, where were they?

I slept, off and on. Each time I woke I would be stronger, and I would always ask about my family. Their answers were always the same. Mom was in a different room and silence regarding Daddy and Katie. Finally, after three days of evasive answers I blurted out, "They're dead, aren't they? Why can't you just tell me?" and then I cried because the look on Aunt Shirley's face said all I needed to know.

Momma died a few hours later.

Physically, I recovered quickly. I read the police report. An intoxicated person had hit us while doing about 70 mph and literally driven her car over the top of ours, mostly over the driver's side. Daddy and Katie had taken the brunt of it, their necks had been broken when the roof crushed down onto their heads. Momma and I had both been thrown forward. My head contacted the back of her soft seat but had hit with such velocity that I have been knocked unconscious. Momma's head made contact with the dash. The subsequent swelling and trauma were too much for her. She never regained consciousness.

And that, Forrest Gump, is all I got to say about that.

I had to blink away a few tears after recounting that event in my life. It had shaped so much that followed it, and the loss of them all is still an open wound. I have to distract myself by looking at the road again, and that is a dangerous mind-set. Let me compose myself a bit. I will get back to you.

3

A Troubled Teen

Was I traumatized? Well, of course I was traumatized! How could I not be? I went to live with my Aunt Shirley, her husband Brad and their three children. Aunt Shirley was the youngest of Momma's family and hence her children were younger than me. Among them, I stuck out like a sore thumb, and everyone... everyone in the entire town seemed to know what had happened to my family and pity oozed out of their eyes, mouths, and actions like suffocating tar. I stopped going to church. I couldn't see their faces or hear their well-meant words of encouragement. I hate those words "sorry for your loss. Really? You're sorry for my loss? I didn't lose something; they were taken from me!"

Obviously, I bounced between deep depression and violent anger. And everyone around me got a good taste of both. Now, Aunt Shirley and Uncle Brad wanted to help me. I knew even then that they did. But I just pushed them away. The harder that they tried, the harder I rejected them. At the same time, they needed to protect their own children from my negative influence. So, they set me up with my very first therapist and I hated them for it.

The doctor's name was Mitchell Burk. He was one of those guys who tries to connect with teenagers by personally relating. In other words, he used a lot of phrases like, "I've been there, man." "Oh, a man has to do what a man has to do." And my personal favorite, "You know that girls don't like moody guys, right?" He would follow that last one up with a wink or a slap on the shoulder. He was incredibly annoying. I got the impression that he wanted to go back in time and be a teenager again, but that would never happen except in his own mind.

Mitch, that's what I had to call him, was a gym nut and his body, he claimed was his temple. You couldn't prove that to me. I often caught him snacking on something decidedly not good for the human body and his trash can always had at least one empty bag of chips or a candy wrapper in it. All of that to the wayside, the girls certainly seemed to buy his particular brand of bull shit.

I saw Mitch every Tuesday and Thursday, except once. He postponed my Thursday session to take his car into the shop and set me up with a Friday session, which he promptly forgot about, not the car, he forgot about our session. When I showed up for my session, he was completely caught off his game. When I got to his office, he had already been standing and had obviously been on his way out. He sputtered a bit but recovered quickly. "Hey, I'm glad you're finally here. I was thinking we could get a bite to eat, you know change the scenery and... umm... relax a bit. Whatcha say, wanna get a burger or something?" Well, I was along for the ride. Going out to an early dinner with Mitch meant that I didn't have to go home and suffer through some more looks from Aunt Shirley and Uncle Brad that bounced from pity to disappointment and even anger so quickly that my head ached.

We stopped at a fast-food place, the kind that has tables inside and out and served mostly burgers and dogs with a large variety of house special type drinks. They had waitresses in short pink or yellow dresses that came to the outside tables. If you ate inside, you got your own from the counter. We sat outside. A cute little blond came up to our table. She was probably 16. At first, I thought that Mitch hadn't actually forgotten our session. I thought that maybe he had just been nervous because he was going to try to set me up with this girl. But the girl was not looking at me. She and Mitch were making doe eyes at each other. He was literally old enough to be her father.

We ordered some burger combinations and in a ploy that he had forgotten something he grabbed her hand as she turned away and while slipping a scrap of paper into her hand, he asked her to take the onions off of his burger. She folded her fingers around that scrap of paper, smiled from ear to ear and quickly retreated. They were as subtle as a boiled egg fart in Church.

When she came back 15 or so minutes later toting our burgers, she was still beaming. Clearly, the contents of the note had been something that she wanted to hear. She dropped my basket of food in front of me and leaned down to place the basket in front of Mitch. The front of her dress drooped just enough to give him a clear view of her scant cleavage, such as it was. Mitch's eyes took in the view with appreciation.

After the girl had finally departed, we ate like two men on completely different missions. I found my burger and fries to be good enough to eat with some appreciation, but I have never been a fast eater, unless there was a need. Mitch on the other hand, devoured his food as if he had not eaten in a week and knew not where he might find another meal in the foreseeable future. The waitress had, of course, slipped a note into his basket, which he retrieved and read as clumsily as he had passed his own note.

Conversation was disjointed. He asked superficial questions regarding how my life was going and barely listened to the answers. He finished his meal quickly, as I said, and once he was done, he became quite antsy. His eyes darting from the amount of food left in my basket to glances in the direction of the burger shop doors, from which the waitresses usually emerged, and down to his watch. Part of me wanted to drag out his agony and eat even slower, while part of me was disgusted that this man was so keen to make his rendezvous with a teenager that he would make a farce out of providing me with proper counselling. In the end, it was the disgust that won. I pushed what was left of my dinner away from me and declared that I was done. Mitch could not hide the glee in his eyes. Soon his torment would be ended, and his true hunger would be satiated, and I would not have changed. My pain would remain. The hollow pit in my being would not be filled and I would continue to trudge through life day by day with the cloud of depression over my head.

Thankfully, my time under the care of Mitchell Burk was short. He was found out when the girls in his life began to talk to each other. How that happened, I really do not know, nor do I care. It is one thing to be a womanizer, I have known many, but to be a womanizer who really only likes teenagers, well now, that is a different story all together. He got what was coming to him and I was glad for it. But it did mean that I was assigned a new counsellor. This time it was a woman. What exactly does an angry teenage boy have to say to a woman?

Geraldine Houck was her name. She was a woman in her forties, who had been married and divorced and had two children at home. Her children were just a few years younger than me, so unlike Mitch, Ms. Houck actually did have some experience dealing with more than just the raging hormones of a teenager. What's more, she actually seemed to care about me, or at least about helping me.

Unfortunately, thanks to Mitch, I had added mistrust to my repertoire of over-the-top emotions. So, even though I had been in therapy for nearly a year, Ms. Houck and I got off to a rocky start. Trust had to be earned, and to a certain degree, Ms. Houck did gain my trust. While she was doing so, I still got into a lot of trouble. I still did well in school, somehow, I could not bring myself to get bad grades based on test results. It would be like flipping my mother off. It would be a personal disgrace if I were to perform at a level less than my absolute best in school. That being said, my grades did eventually suffer when I discovered alcohol and marijuana, both of which muddled my brain and gave me a convenient excuse to cut school. How could I go to school if I could not seem to wake up in the morning?

It was during this time in my life that I began to act out in a more public fashion. I became a delinquent. My parents and sister would have been so ashamed of the teenager that I had become. But for some reason, I could not shake it. One bad decision led to another, until one winter night I was both intoxicated and high on marijuana, and I found myself slipping, sliding, and stumbling down a snow-covered street just after sundown, with only one thought in my mind, "I have to get home." I had to find my way back to my life. I did not know where I was nor how I had come to be there. I only knew the one thought, so when I spied an older woman climbing into a car in her driveway, I ran to her, not to help, not to find comfort, but to push her down onto the icy driveway and to rip her keys from her hand. I jumped into the car. While slamming the door, it caught on something and instead of looking down to identify the obstacle I simply pushed my left foot out of the door with considerable force, connected with something and kicked it away. I jammed the keys into the ignition and turned it with such force that the key twisted in the lock, but the car started. My heart jumped with joy, now I could go home. I backed the car out of the driveway and turned it into the street, but when I hit the gas, the car did not race down the street, instead it lurched and spun on the icy snow. It spun in circles until it stopped with a crash against another car. My head only saw the events of that other day, the day when my life had been stolen from me. Through the fog of drugs and alcohol I felt it all over again. I do not remember screaming or getting out of the car and yelling for my parents and Katie at the top of my lungs. I have no memory of the old woman laying like a lifeless lump in the gutter, she must have rolled down the driveway, or of the man who came to her side. I have a disconnected memory of that man yelling in my face to shut up and demanding to know what I had done and then hitting me hard enough to shut off my lights.

I awoke in the hospital. But the room was not like any hospital room that I had ever seen. It was small and sparse. I tried to sit up, but the clanking new bracelet on my wrist stopped me with just the sound. The new bracelet was attached to both me and the bed. Before I could make any sense of how I had gotten to that place, the door opened, and a nurse dressed in a traditional white outfit that was accented with pink entered the room. Behind her was a man in a police uniform. He looked at me with cold angry eyes and the door shut behind the nurse.

I tried to find out from her what had happened and why I was at the hospital. She told me that I was there for observation while I detoxed, but there was nothing more that she could tell me. I would need to wait for my attorney. That is when some of the events from the previous night began to come back, and my heart sank in my chest. What had I done?

I remembered that I had shoved that woman to the ground and that I had heard and felt bones breaking as I pulled the keys from her hand. A hand that had clenched in pain as her frail body had impacted the unforgiving ground. I remembered that I had glanced at the obstacle that had been blocking the door, the silver head of the woman, and I had kicked her in the face to get her out of the way and finally I had remembered that as I had backed out of the driveway, I had felt the car go over something. The reality of what I had become crashed down on top of me. I had only wanted to go home, back to my real life. But this was my real life, and I was a monster that spread hurt and pain like peanut butter all over everyone that I touched. What would my parents and Katie think?

I allowed depression and sorrow to fill me. I lay for hours like a lost soul as the nurse came and went. She brought food, but I could not eat. I asked her once if the lady was alright. She glared at me and walked out without replying. I was too ashamed to cry, but I still wallowed in self-pity. Just after the nurse brought my dinner, I assumed it was dinner by the items on the plate, my aunt and uncle came into the room, followed by a man in a crisp tailored suit, a lawyer, I presumed. The disappointment written on Aunt Shirley's face was almost too much to bear, but I had to bear it because it was honest.

Aunt Shirley fussed about the handcuffs and how I was being treated. Uncle Brad told her to stop because it was what I deserved. I asked them about the woman. That is when the attorney started to talk. He started by telling me that she was in the hospital, in intensive care. Much of what happened to me in the coming days and weeks would be determined by what happened to her. He asked me who I had spoken to since waking and what I remembered about what happened the night before. At the urging of Aunt Shirley, I told him an abridged, detached version of everything. My aunt was both shocked and disappointed while Uncle Brad was just angry. Then the attorney, Samuel Manyfeathers, told me what was going to happen next. If the woman, Mrs. Susan Hasse lived, I would be charged with attempted murder. He would try to plea that down to reckless endangerment. If Mrs. Hasse died, then I would be charged with murder. He would try to plea that down to reckless endangerment that resulted in loss of life. The other thing that had yet to be decided was if they were going to charge me as a child or an adult because I was so close to my 18th birthday. Mr. Manyfeathers figured that I would be charged as an adult and when I was convicted, I would go to prison. Aunt Shirley started crying. Uncle Brad tried to comfort her by telling her that I was strong and would likely survive prison. The only good news that came out of that conversation was that I learned that I had run over a package that Mrs. Hasse had been carrying and not Mrs. Hasse. The tires had crushed her three-year-old great-great-grandchild's birthday toy and not Mrs. Hasse's head.

The next day, the sheriff's deputy came and took me to jail, where I would await trial. Aunt Shirley wanted me to come home, but Uncle Brad and I both wanted me to stay in jail. Doing so would mean that I would be safe from public outcry. Mrs. Hasse was an 81-year-old woman who had strong ties to the community and given it was a relatively small town, she knew nearly everyone. I had become a pariah overnight. As far as I was concerned, I deserved to be in jail. I deserved to be hung.

The days passed like molasses in January while I awaited my fate. One day a man came to see me. I remembered him as the man that had hit me that night and stopped my drug and alcohol induced rampage. He was Jens Hasse, the grandson of Mrs. Hasse. I was still sweating out my addictions, but for the first time since the death of my family, my mind was clear, and I was ready to face life without them. Mr. Hasse told me that his grandmother was improving. Her bones were healing, and she had opened her eyes and could recognize her family and that she was in the hospital. So, brain trauma was not a factor. Her jaw had been wired shut because I had fractured it. Her hand was in a full soft cast because they had needed to perform surgery to correct the damage that I had caused. Her tailbone had cracked and twisted when I had thrown her to the ground. It was a common injury when people landed on their asses from a slip. It would correct itself. Considering what I had done, Mrs. Hasse was in relatively good condition. It had been my kick to her face and the subsequent snapping back of the neck that had put her in ICU.

I told Mr. Hasse that I could not apologize enough, that there were no words that could correct my actions. He agreed. He wanted me to know that his family knew about what had happened to mine. His grandmother had been sympathetic to the entire ordeal and to me specifically. That news made me feel even worse. She had told her family most recently that she wondered and prayed if she could do anything to help me to find my way. Mr. Hasse was wondering if what had happened between his grandmother and me might be an answer to her prayer. I was dumbfounded. I had never imagined that anyone would give a damn about me, other than my aunt who was obligated to care. When I think back on my overall thought processes of that time, I am amazed that I survived with anyone at my side. My aunt was not obligated to love me or care about me, but I was so convinced that I was unworthy of any kind of compassion that I pushed everyone away from me. The ultimate lesson of that time for me can be summed up with this: Self-pity is a terrible deep dark hole that anyone can become lost in. It takes someone who really wants to live to dig themselves out of it.

When Mr. Hasse suggested that my horrible deeds were in some way an answer to a prayer, I could not believe my ears. His final words to me that day still echo in my head, "I know my grandmother. When she awakes, she will want to talk to you." And that my dear friends, terrified me.

And so, she did. Six weeks later, they took the wires out of her jaw. A few weeks after that and I was taken from jail to her bedside. She was bedridden at home. When I arrived at her home, in the sheriff's car, the same place that I had originally met Mrs. Hasse in the driveway, I could see the crowd of concerned citizens in her yard. I half expected to be torn limb from limb before I could ever see her. But that is not what happened. The deputy opened my car door, and the townsfolk created a path for us to walk up to Mrs. Hasse's front door. No one said a word to me. The house door opened before me, and I was escorted by family to Mrs. Hasse's bedside.

My aunt and uncle were already there, and several people that I did not recognize. No one was speaking in this room either. I felt like I was visiting some kind of Queen, and maybe I was, I don't really know. What I do know is that Mrs. Hasse was and is one of the most gracious and generous people that has ever graced this world with her presence. She was on par with Mother Teresa and just as worthy of sainthood. She asked me to tell her why I had attacked her and taken her car. I started out slow, but then a dam broke inside of me, and I told her everything, from the moment that I learned that my family was dead to the day that I knelt bawling my eyes out at her bedside. I left nothing out. I told her about my pain, and my emptiness. I told her about my anger and self-loathing, and I told her about how much my aunt really loves me and wants to help but that because she looks so much like my mother I hurt every time I looked at her. I laid my heart bear and cried until there was no water left in me, and the whole while, Mrs. Hasse stroked my hair or held my hand. In the end, I apologized profusely knowing all the while that no words would ever be good enough and that is when she said, "Then let your actions be your apology." I looked up at her with red puffy wet eyes and asked her "How?" She told me, "Serve our God, serve our country and serve the people that live here. Be the shield between angry, hurt young men and the innocent. Be the rock that crushes those who would harm the weak, the young and the innocent. Be the example that your parents, that your father was to you and make yourself proud to look in the mirror."

That was the day that I became a boy that was on the path to manhood. I think that I am still working on being a real man, but I am closer now than I have ever been.

A few weeks later, we all came before Judge Dillon Hasse, yes, they're related, I told you it was a small town, but with the insistence of my aunt and uncle, Mr. Manyfeathers waived the "conflict of interest" clause and Judge Hasse saw the case of the angry young man vs. Mrs. Susan Hasse. It was a short trial, Mrs. Hasse would drop all charges on the condition that young Mr. Steven W. Harrington would join the Army and pay for all damages to her car and would write to her at least once a month to report on his progress until Mrs. Hasse should pass on to the other side.

I was a bit torn when the Judge said "Army," I had always imagined that I would join the Navy like my father. But as I stood there with the conflict of hurting her, then her giving me a second chance... I was sure that she would not be angry if I asked to go into the Navy instead, and yet, in my heart I felt unworthy. I was not my father and I had disgraced his name. I did not deserve to be in the Navy and pretend that I had earned the honor of walking in his footsteps. So, in the end, I stayed silent and did the only honorable thing that I could do, I accepted my punishment as the judge saw fit to dole it out and was signed up for the Army. I was not surprised that a local Army recruiter was on hand to sign me up personally, and yes, his last name was Hasse as well.

Mrs. Hasse has been gone now for sixteen years. She lived eighty-five years and died just two weeks shy of her eighty-sixth birthday. I still write her letters. I seal them in envelopes addressed to Heaven and place them in the box that has the lock of my sister's hair, my parents wedding rings, all of Mrs. Hasse's letters to me, that token from my first kill and other important keepsakes of my life. I am going to need a bigger box.

For those sixteen years when I wrote to her, at first, I told her how I was progressing through basic. I did not tell her how hard it was; I had not earned the right to complain about my own pain. I was being punished. So, I took it like a man. It wasn't until I went on my first deployment as an Army grunt that I remembered what she had said in that bedroom so long ago. I was to be the barrier, the blockade, the man that stood up to tyranny to save the innocent, not the petulant little boy who looked at the Army like a prison cell. I think that is when I grew some eyes and really took responsibility for what I had done and who I had become. I told her all of that in one of my letters and when she responded, I could see the dried water drops on her otherwise pristine stationary. She told me in that letter something that I had not known, she not only had known my parents, but she had also watched them grow up, and that we were related to the Hasses just like everyone else in that town. Somehow, it did not surprise me.

My shame melted away after reading that letter. My relationship with Mrs. Hasse grew into a friendship. I shared everything with her, even my first encounter with Patti. She chided me for my shyness and told me to, "stop beating myself up. The past is gone, all any of us has is the future." It was odd, I could talk to any girl in the world, except Patti. When I told her that, I could feel her head shake. I don't know how I could have gotten through those first years without her friendship and guidance.

All I can say about all of that is, God sure does know how to make lemonade out of lemons, and he knows how to heal a broken heart. Mrs. Hasse once wrote that, "out of hardship comes strength and out of pain comes healing." I don't know how strong I am, or how healed I am, but I do know that Mrs. Hasse forgave me and from that forgiveness came love and respect from me to her and pride and thankfulness from her to me.

What happened to my aunt and uncle? Well, not long after the trial, about a year later my Aunt Shirley divorced Brad. He had wanted me sent to prison and just would not let it all go. So, she let him go and raised their children alone. I sent them money, after I finished paying for the repairs on Mrs. Hasse's car and eventually, Aunt Shirley met a man who was worthy of her. I am still close to her and her family.

—----

The road is still empty. I wonder if anyone uses this damn road on a regular basis. The snow has already stopped. A light dusting of powder covers me, my spotter, and my rifle. More camouflage. Sometimes I do wonder what happened to that jackass Brad. But he is unimportant to me, just an idol curiosity. For some reason, every time I think of Uncle Brad I think of boot camp. Maybe it is because while I was in boot camp, I really wanted to just punch the man. I fantasized about it. Of course, he would have kicked my ass, at least when I started boot camp, but maybe not so much afterwards. Maybe because Uncle Brad was a bully and a not-so-nice man and I met a few of those in boot camp. Let me tell you about it.

4

Boot Camp

When I first started boot camp, I was both excited and scared out of my shoes. It is easy acting tough and daring when you are drunk or high. But when the chemicals wear off, you are left with just you. They aren't lying when they say, "Have a drink of courage" and hand you a shot of something strong. The problem is that bravado is just that, bravado. It only has teeth if you can back it up and I most certainly could not as an 18-year-old boy.

I had signed up for Army Infantry, or MOS 11B. That means that I got sent to Fort Benning in Georgia. All I can say is that I could not have picked a worse time to get sent to Georgia. By the time the trial was over, and the paperwork was done, it was late spring. Do you know what Georgia is like in late spring? No, well let me tell you, it is just starting to get hot. The first batch of mosquitos are having a heyday hatching and looking for food. And this skinny white boy, apparently had some really tasty blood.

Don't get me wrong, Georgia is beautiful. It is green and colorful and warm and humid. And the wisteria trees drape like royal cascades of jewels over streets, walkways, and houses, lending a dreamy appearance to everything. The houses, in the older sections of Columbus, the city nearest to Fort Benning are magnificent. I could sit on a street bench for hours just looking at the houses before me and imagining the people who once lived in these glorious edifices of human imagination and engineering. I am transported back a century in time when I have time to just sit and look. Unfortunately, as a new recruit, I had very little of that, time, that is.

Fort Benning sits on the boarder of Alabama and Georgia, but is officially in Georgia. It opened for training in WWI and has grown into the main Army training place. I have gone back twice in my career. Once to get my sniper training and once to go to Officer Training School after I got my degree. Right now, I am going to tell you a little bit about my first time in Fort Benning. My time in basic training, or boot camp.

I was a skinny boy at eighteen. I had never really been out for too much in sports, so I had remained rather skinny in school. The one sport that I did enjoy was swimming. That came from my father's influence, he was not much of a swimmer, and hence why he was an electrician on his PT boat and not in the actual swim to the island squad. But that inspired me to learn how to swim and to do it well. Not because I wanted to best my old man, but because it seemed like something he might have done prior to entering the Navy had he known how much he would need it. Remember, my plan was to enter the Navy, eventually.

Being a swimmer made me lean and strong, but still quite skinny and that little attribute made me a bit of a target for the other boys, especially the "corn-fed farmers" that looked like they could bench press a full-grown heifer. It was a lot like high school all over again. I was the smart one and one of the smallest. But I had learned from my high school experience, I only showed my intelligence on paper, well... when they let me. Boot camp is a bit different.

All boot camps have stages that recruits must go through to advance to the next stage. Failing at one is called a wash out and you have to repeat the stage. No one wants a wash out on their record. One would think that infantry should be the easiest boot camp to get through. On one hand, they are right but on the other, they are dead wrong. Infantry is about 80% physical and 20% mental. Which is the exact opposite of me.

At first, as I said, the focus was on the physical. The instructors needed their recruits to be strong and to have stamina. So, we were up before the sun and out doing something physical. It usually started with a five-mile run, then back to camp to do sit-ups, push-ups, chin-ups and a whole slew of other "ups." Everyone had trouble with something. As long as we were running and doing all of our "ups" with only body weight, I held my own, but of course, after week two, they started adding weight and a lot of it.

After one particular morning about two weeks in and a thirty-pound ruck on my back, I was shot. We had been at it all week because there are no days off in boot camp, not in the beginning anyway. After a hastily eaten breakfast, we went back to the barracks to shower so we could go to class and that is when I ran into the wall of corn-fed boys. Now they weren't after me in particular. I had been holding my own, but I wasn't one of them either. They were having a go at some other boys. It all went something like this, I walked in on Bruce, Matt and Phil, the corn-fed squad, giving Tom and Terrance, the two having the most trouble and often falling out of Physical Training or PT some of their own brand of counselling.

Bruce, (top corn-fed), "You're makin' us look bad, ya little punk!" He was nose to nose with Terrance who was about 5'6" and 110 soaking wet. Bruce was an easy 6' and about 200 pounds of farm hardened muscle. Bruce gave Terrance a shove and the poor boy hit the concrete floor hard and skidded about three feet. That's when Matt shoved Tom and landed him next to Terrance. Tom was the white version of Terrance, small and skinny. But Tom was also an introvert. How he got into the Army was a mystery to me. I had never spoken to either. In fact, I had only said a few words in passing to any of the five boys present. So, when I walked in, I was not exactly welcomed.

"What the fuck do you want, pencil?" Matt demanded when I came in. "Pencil" is what they called me. I was about 5'8" and about 160 at that time, but I did hold my own in PT. So, I had avoided this kind of public confrontation and humiliation.

I shook my head to the question but did not leave.

Matt, "Just came to watch, heh?"

Bruce, "Just stay out of it, Pencil. Right?"

When I said nothing, Matt pressed the question, "He said, stay out of it. Dintcha hear him?"

I nodded like a jackass and slid around them to my own bunk. What was I going to do? There were three of them, twice my size and looking for a fight. Tom and Terrance needed to stand up for themselves.

Neither boy had moved from their inglorious spots on the floor. Tom was crying and Terrance looked like he wanted to run home to his mother. Maybe he did. Neither looked in my direction. Why should they? I had made it clear that they would get no help from me. So much for the promise to be the barricade. Yeah, that's what I thought at the time too. But I also could not see a way to be that barricade, not yet anyway. I was still learning how this all worked.

A few other boys started to filter into the barracks. We didn't have a lot of time to shower and get to class. Each time that Tom or Terrance moved to get up, one of the corn-fed would push them back down and say things like, "You get to wait until the men have showered. You think we want little fairies like you looking at our dicks while we're in the shower?" Everyone filtering in, quickly made stock of the scene and did as I had done, skirt around them to get their shower gear.

This went on for three days. After breakfast we would find Tom and Terrance sitting on the floor waiting for everyone else to shower and leave before they could get up and do the same. No one spoke to them. Did the sergeant of the barracks know? Of course, he knew, how could he not? Bruce was the Top Cadet in the barracks, which made him the hall monitor or the teacher's pet. Use whatever adjective you want to describe him. With him at the head of this intimidation squad we all figured that whatever they did it was sanctioned by the real powers in the camp.

On day four, Tom and Terrance started showing signs of physical abuse. Black eyes, split lips, and finger-like bruising on their thin arms. Meanwhile, those of us who had been watching and doing nothing were splitting into two clear groups, those who seemed to accept it all as a matter of course and those who were uncomfortable with it all. I was in the latter group.

Five days in and the Sergeant came into the tent and saw the boys on the floor while we all did nothing. He looked at the boys and scanned the room, looking each of us in the eyes before turning around and walking out. Bruce and the corn-feds looked very smug and proud of themselves. They saw what the Sergeant did, or rather did not do, as clear affirmation of what they were doing. So did a lot of other guys. The split in the barracks began to shift. More people were joining the matter of course group and abandoning their moral values. I was not one of them. In fact, when the Sergeant had looked into my eyes, I had not seen any kind of affirmation for what they were doing, what I saw was a question, "Are you man enough to do something?"

Six days in and Tom and Terrance were both bloody before morning PT. They were clearly injured and yet still trying to keep up. That is when I finally grew a pair and dropped back to encourage them. They looked at me like I was taunting them. I wanted to just pull away and leave them to their fate, but my father's voice inside my head would no longer be silent, and Mrs. Hasse's voice was screaming. So, I stayed at their sides through the run. When we got back to camp for all of the other PT, I stayed with them and helped them as best I could. And when the corn-feds came over to start on them again, I was now included in their tirade.

Bruce, "Look everyone, Pencil has joined the fairy squad. What'd they do, suck your cock?"

Phil approached me, he was the biggest and the dumbest of the crew. He reached out as if he was going to clamp my throat in his hand. I dodged him and slapped his hand away. A general gasp went through the group. The Sergeant folded his arms across his barrel chest and watched.

"How dare you hit one of us?!" Matt bellowed and charged me. He literally picked me up off of the ground and was going to body slam me. But he had grabbed me by my waist, that meant that I was literally above his head and had two free hands, so I boxed his ears. He howled and dropped me in favor of grabbing his own head. When he took his hands from his ears, blood was trickling out of them. I had popped his ear drums and in doing so made him very angry, but also very wobbly on his feet. His equilibrium was gone. I easily avoided his next charge and with a shove, I landed him on his side in the grass.

Meanwhile, Phil had recovered from his initial shock of being slapped. I am fairly certain that no one but his mother, if anyone, had slapped Phil in a very long time. Bruce just stood there dumbfounded while Phil wanted to charge me and plant me into the ground, but a side glance at Matt made him rethink his strategy. While the two lunkheads were contemplating their next move, I took the opportunity to open my mouth.

"Look guys, these two may be small, but they are here. After all the shit you have rained down on them, they are still here. That has to say something." I looked around at the faces that had encircled us. I had their attention, now what do I say? My father's face flicked into my mind and the image of Mrs. Hasse in the gutter. I took a deep breath and said, "We're here to train. To learn and to build a unit with each other. If we go into battle tomorrow, how do you think Tom and Terrance are going to react... not to the enemy, but to us? Are they going to have our backs? Did we have theirs?" I let that last sentence hang on its own for a long minute. I gestured at the corn-fed squad, who had all huddled around the injured Matt. "Do we really want these guys to be our leaders? I don't." The faces started to respond to what I was saying. I pointed at two of the guys that had been in the "uncomfortable" group. "Why don't you two take Tom and Terrance to Medical?" It was more of a statement than a question. Then I turned to Bruce and Phil. "Take Matt to Medical." That was an order. No one moved. "Well, get on with it! I want to eat before the day starts and you are wasting all of our time!" My momma used to say that to me when I was slow to get out of bed in the morning and it worked on these guys just like it had worked on me. Everyone started moving. I looked at the Sergeant. He had been joined by several other sergeants and a lieutenant. They were mumbling to each other. I turned and headed towards the mess hall and was surprised to see the remainder of our barracks following me.

After that little encounter, I was the unofficial leader of our barracks, not that I was actually leading anything, but they all followed where I went anyway. Matt was in the hospital for a really long time and was washed back to the beginning. Tom also had to stay in the hospital. He had three broken ribs where someone's foot had connected with his rib cage. He was also washed back to the beginning. They were not put into the same barracks again. The rest of us continued on, with me in the lead. I had no idea what the hell I was doing. So, I focused on the physical for several weeks, until everyone was at least not limping through half the shit. Then, I personally started going to the gym and doing a lot of resistance training when I could make the time. Others started to join me; Terrance was one of them. Although he never really put on a lot of poundage, he did get considerably stronger.

I had no need to really focus on the mental part of things, my mother had taught me how to study and how to learn. I guess others never got that kind of upbringing, so I helped them.

The Sergeant never spoke to me about our little fight. He just started treating me like I was in charge, under him of course. When he told me to assemble the men, I did so. When he told me to discipline someone, I did so... but not like the corn-feds had done. I did it the old-fashioned way, I handed them a toothbrush and told them to scrub the floor, even the shower and bathroom. Speaking of the bathroom, here is a little fact about Basic Training that no one really talks about.

We have lots of toilets, there is no shortage, but only one stall has a roll of toilet paper. Everyone is so uptight in the first two to three weeks that the single roll of toilet paper doesn't lose a single square. In fact, in our group one of the guys didn't take a shit for almost six weeks. He finally had to go to the medical unit to get his bowels evacuated. See how that bit of knowledge swims around in your brain for a minute, and then we'll get back to the story. Now you can appreciate why my form of discipline always seemed to do the trick.

By the time we got to the final stage of boot camp, we were as well-oiled a team as can be expected of a bunch of boys who are just learning how to be men. Come to find out that the corn-fed boys weren't really from the country. They let us assume what we wanted. They were actually from the big city and were accustomed to being bullies. The actual country boys hung out with the surfers and were really laid back. Anyway, Bruce and Phil decided that it was better for them if they learned to get along and actually became valued members of our team, especially when we had competitions with the other barracks. Who knew that Phil could spin a rifle like that? The control and the smooth transitions between one move and the next were truly beautiful. Even so, Phil didn't have the brains to be anything but infantry, but he was good at it. And Bruce was the best anchor anyone could have in any tug of war contest. He made a great infantryman. Terrance turned out to be incredibly fast when he finally got into shape. It also turned out that Terrance was pretty smart and ended up going into communications when he graduated boot camp. Tom was really affected by the bullying, so as soon as he graduated, he sent himself to college and got a degree in business administration and then went into Officer Candidate's school. I think he still got bullied, but maybe in a different more playful kind of way.

Boot camp was hard, and I would not have missed it for the world. I wrote to Mrs. Hasse every week. I admit it was hard during that week when I was being a coward while others were being abused, but I did write her. It was a load of mush and crap with no details at all and yes, she called me on it. She asked, "Are you so tired that you cannot write me a proper letter?" She knew something was wrong. So, the next week, after I had boxed Matt's ears, I wrote and told her everything that had happened. You know what she wrote back, of course you don't, but I am going to tell you. She said, "And so you have started the journey at last, the journey between being a selfish boy to becoming a caring and thoughtful man. I knew that you had it in you, Steven, because that is who your parents were. They were kind, hardworking, loving, and caring people. I think that they would be proud of the new direction that you are taking." I cried when I read those words.

I was still a far cry from what I became, but this was where I started making those changes. I still wonder if the Sergeant would have stepped in had the "corn-feds" not backed off after I hurt Matt. I would probably not have survived a beating from the three of them. But that is something that we will never know.

When I look in the mirror now, the skinny Pencil is long gone. I grew some more in my early twenties and am now 6'1" and 210. I am proud to say that I am pretty cut and do attract a lot of female attention. And yes, sometimes I strut like a peacock, but Patti pinches me and brings me back to reality and yes, we make a very pretty couple, if I do say so myself. My eyes are hazel, my father's eyes were green and so were Katie's and my mothers were a beautiful shade of blue. My hair is light brown with some reddish highlights, and I am very white, like an Irishman, like my mother's side of the family. To be fair, Daddy's family is pretty white too, he was of German and

Scottish descent while Momma was Irish and French well, not really French. They just lived in France; they were from Austria. So, lots of Germanic tribe and Viking going on, so really white. At least I do not burn as easy in the sun as my sister did. I am not ashamed of being white. It is who I am. I cannot change it. I can only be what my parents and Mrs. Hasse want me to be, a good man.

I cannot help but grin when I remember boot camp. I kept track of a lot of the guys through the years and even ran into a few of them. Most have already retired or just got out. Matt made a full recovery. But broken ear drums never quite heal right, and he will have ringing in his ears his whole life. Tom went on to become that Officer I was telling you about. I guess he was good at it. But he was in one of the towers on 9-11.

With that memory, I take an unusually long pull of air and hold it. The clouds are still hanging low, heavy with water. Lots of more snow to come. The road is glistening with it. I bet it is slick as hell. A couple of birds off to my right are having an argument. They are squawking at each other and flying around each other erratically, sometimes openly attacking. They will get over it soon and fly away to find a different battle ground. For the moment, it is a nice distraction.

5

Our Team

So much for how I got into this man's Army. Let's get back to funnier stories. I told you a bit about Patti, it's only right that I should tell you a bit about Doug too. Through the years, Doug and I became inseparable. We pulled each other out of more scrapes than I care to remember, both in the field and at home.

Douglas Kaelan Shelby came to the Army from the Marines. He had the body of Atlas, although quite a bit shorter, and a no-nonsense Marine exterior complete with the high and tight and a perpetual frown. This usually kept people from approaching him with any kind of confidence. It was not a reciprocal behavior, after all, he was the one to approach Patti and let's face it; they fit like a hand in a glove.

A person had to get to know Doug to get to his sense of humor, which, like most of us in this career field was a bit twisted and a lot like gallows humor. Although, unlike the cops, our sense of humor was a bit darker. Cops, military, or civilian all tend to lean on a watered-down version of gallows humor, and they pepper their jokes with sexual innuendo and homosexual hints, that is, until they have actually been in the shit. Once that happens, their humor becomes true gallows humor because they have seen the dead, helped make them dead or had to fight for their lives. Then their humor is not so funny anymore. I don't care what anyone says, killing someone or running for your life changes a person. Now when I say, "see the dead," I'm not talking about great aunt Betty who died in her sleep, although that can screw with your head, it is nothing like going to a disaster zone and seeing bloated bodies floating in the water or walking into a living horror story like Auschwitz where emaciated bodies are stacked like cord wood and open graves contain thousands... not dozens of ravaged bodies. We live in America and for the most part, civilians don't see shit like that, but some cops... they do see shit like that, and it changes them. That's when they understand what the folks in the military have to deal with in foreign countries and that's when their humor takes a turn towards the dark side.

Anyway, Doug had gallows humor with a lot of innuendo thrown in just to pepper the gravy. For instance, when Doug walks into the room, regardless of who was in the room, he starts with, "What's up, fuckers?" the conversation would usually go downhill from there. He often steers the conversation towards some kind of homosexual direction, often by asking someone, it could be anyone really, about their "gay sex life." The conversation would go something like this:

Doug, "What's up, fuckers?"

General greeting, "How's it going, fucker?"

Doug, "So, Dusty, did you get a ladder so you can give it to Beaner... you know better?" He says this while holding his arms up like he is holding something at hip height and then he starts thrusting his hips to get the point across.

Dusty, "Yeah, I only needed one of those step things that they use in 'Step-exercise'. I mean look at him," Gesturing towards Al, his partner, i.e., Beaner. "He's not that much taller than me."

Doug, "Ahh... I see, that's a fair point." Turning to Al, i.e., Beaner, "So is sex better now between you?"

Al, "It could be better." Dusty gasps in mock shock. "Well, you really do have a tough time holding on with those T-Rex arms of yours."

General laughter, then Jake says, "Maybe you could get a rope?"

Steven, "Maybe hay hooks, for a better grip."

General consent, and the conversation gets moved to a different person until finally Bryce butts in with, "Okay, enough. Let's get down to business." And everyone shuts up, except Doug, who must have the last word. "What? Too much for you? Feeling puny?" He gets a glare and shuts up.

All the guys in our team had that humor, that's because we have all been there and done that... but that is never what we talk about with anyone but each other... and a few trusted folks that we consider family... but we never talk about that stuff with our wives or loved ones or even the well-meaning psychologist that we all get assigned to us at some point to fix us. It is just too damn scary for them, and they will never understand. Men that tell their wives, usually get divorced soon after. I really think maybe that they do not want to be understood they just want an excuse to be angry and that is what breaks up the marriage.

When we have an audience, we joke about stupid stuff and throw in a lot of innuendo. We rib Doug about his weak chin and how he tries to compensate for it by working out.

He just tells us to go fuck ourselves and then ribs on Dustin for his short arms and how they had to modify a rifle made for a two-year-old so he could reach the trigger. Dustin then turns the joke on Alejandro and wants to know how in hell Al managed to convince local PD to take him back to the party that he had wandered away from in a drunken stupor. He was found knocking on a stranger's door at 0300 hours... this was after he had walked into the parked truck in the driveway and picked himself up. The cops took him back to the party... WTF! Everyone wants to know the secret. The personal attacks continue until someone has to leave which generally starts a general exodus or the boss brings us back on point.

We were and are a tight group of men well, to be fair, snipers are only really close to their spotter. The rest of the "team" is the group of men that you are on the same base with, you do train with them, but you spend hours, days and even weeks training with just you and your spotter. The rest of the guys share the same piece of dirt and are training at the same time, but you are with your spotter. There has to be a bond between you. If he breathes different, you need to know what that means, if anything. If something doesn't click between you, then you will not be effective as a team.

Another thing, you are all probably asking, where are the women? There are no female snipers that are deployed as such. Mostly because of the need to stay in one place for such a long time, women have issues with the lack of lavatories and the monthly curse of Montezuma which could cause an issue in that particular style of mission. There is nothing sexist here, just practical. In my experience, women are very good shots, but being a sniper is not just about hitting a target.

There are eight men to a sniper unit, four groups of two. One man is the shooter, the other is the spotter, and it is not uncommon for us to switch it around until you find the right match. Originally, Doug and I were not on the same team. But we swapped guys around and made it so, after we got to know each other. We found that we had more in common and Doug and I clicked, after I got over the idea that he was a Marine. I had reservations about him when he first joined the unit, mostly because he had been a Marine. Jar Heads are notoriously thick headed, and Doug was no different. He was gruff, rude, and tried to insinuate himself into conversations where he wasn't invited. As I got to know him, I realized that he was not such a bad guy. He was a combat vet, which earned him a spot in our unit and a few points of respect, but it was when he took one on the chin for us when the captain caught us being stupid in public... and no, I am not going to tell you what we were doing... that's when he earned our friendship and really became part of the team. Hey, I am not going to tell what we were doing on that particular occasion because frankly, you would not think that it was funny. We thought that it was hysterical, but you would not. We were not hurting anyone, making fun of anyone, or damaging anything, but we were having fun and that is all that you need to know.

The other members of our unit who were snipers were Alejandro Enrique Cano, Dustin Allister Benton, Jake Bradley Sanders, Bryce Wendall Masters, Chase Filipe McDermott, Patrick David Rigsby and me, Steven Washington Harrington. Of the crew, Bryce was the boss. He started out as a lieutenant straight out of Basic, but by the time I joined the team he was a captain. He was a good leader, and he knew what he was about.

Al's nickname was the Bean, obviously because he was of Mexican descent but also because he was a short guy and beans are small. I always found it a bit ironic that Dusty got the short jokes more than the Bean because Dusty was the taller of the two and the jokes always went the other direction. I guess jokes need to just be organic to work. I mean, you know when someone is trying to tell you about something that was so funny when it happened, but it is not so funny in the retelling. Yeah, that's what is called an "organic" joke. You cannot script it. It just happens and it is funny when it happens, but maybe not so much later.

The Bean was a wicked shot and lousy with numbers, so he was usually the shooter for team two. His partner, the man who had been my partner before Doug was Dusty. Al's first partner, the one who Doug replaced, was a guy named Nick. Nick transferred to a different unit in a different state, so he could be closer to his ailing father. Dusty was super smart and had a dry wit. He had been a deputy sheriff at one point in his life, so he was the authority of right and wrong, especially when the team was out drinking. I am not sure how that made his drunken decisions any better than the rest of us, but we went with it.

Jake was the educated redneck and overall lunkhead of the crew. I could never fathom how a man can have so much book smarts and still make idiotic decisions. One time, while on active duty, he called in sick with the stomach flu and then, half an hour later he posted a picture of him and some of his cousins making a booze run, while intoxicated, on social media. You just gotta shake your head and move on. He was the smartest dumb ass that I have ever known. His partner was Bryce. Bryce was the guy who was the most put together, he was, after all, the leader of the crew. That is not to say that he did not have his demons. Bryce had seen more than his fair share of bad stuff and it had affected him in a bad way. He talked a really good game and could back it up in almost any department. But his moral compass was definitely not pointing north. He had been a drug dealer while in high school but changed his evil ways to join the Army and make something of himself. He never went back to selling, but after the first blood bath that he got thrown into, I am pretty sure that his compass got kicked sideways. He started cheating on his wife, who he had married at sixteen and knocked up a month later. She divorced him while we were deployed, and the judge gave her custody of their three children. What little money the child support and alimony left him at the end of each month went to women and booze. While on the job he played it straight and he never did anything to cause command to get involved. Like I said, he was a good leader. It's not like he was the first or last serviceman to become a womanizing alcoholic. Every place that we went, whether it was in hostile territory or in friendly it did not matter, by the second day, Bryce had at least one woman that he was sleeping with. Sometimes it was other service members, most of the time it was a local or three. He did not like shitting where he ate, so he did try to stay away from the service women. But that did mean that he was in the medical tent a lot getting something for his pecker, if you know what I mean. Once, we lost him the second day into a deployment. We did not lose him in the field, we lost him in the compound. So, we went looking for him. We found him in the tent of a prostitute. He was all sorts of messed up, and not just with alcohol. He had three women in bed with him and the room really stunk, in not a good way. Well, we retrieved him and tried to sneak him back into our tent. That was all kinds of messed up. But we did get him there. We gave him a shower in the tent, cuz he couldn't even stand on his own and we didn't want anyone seeing him in this state and he stunk, really bad and we just couldn't stand it. He was out on opium. We had seen the pipes and knowing him, he had not intended to get high on opium, but when the girls lit up he probably got a lot of secondhand smoke from it. Anyway, we had to dry him out and set him square quickly because we were due to go out in three days. We took turns wiping his sweat, gagging him, and holding him down while he dried out. He defecated on himself, and despite being dehydrated, he pissed constantly. We had to burn his cot once we got him figured out. It was a good thing that we had a few medics in the team, cuz he needed an I.V. to help flush him. And all of this was done on the Q.T. no one could know, or he would probably have gotten a dishonorable for conduct unbecoming an officer, and they wouldn't be wrong. But we just couldn't let that happen to Bryce. He hadn't endangered anyone but himself and we could fix that. By day three, just before we were to go out, Bryce woke up from a deep sleep. He found himself in a sweat and piss-soaked cot with us scuttling about the tent packing our shit and his. We urged him to go and get a quick shower so we could head out. He still stunk, even after the shower. Opium comes out through the sweat, kind of like meth does, and it is rancid smelling. Lucky for him, we were on our own on this little party. As far as we know, no one who mattered ever found out and he stayed clean, from booze and women for nearly a year after that incident.

So, as I said, as long as he could stay on point while on mission, he was left to his private life. Now that's not to say that we just let him commit all of this self-inflicted pain without trying to get involved and help him out. He was our brother, but some folks just don't want help and you cannot help someone who doesn't want it. It's like that old saying, you can lead a horse to water, but you can't make them drink. That was Captain Bryce.

Chase was a handsome devil complete with the dark wavy hair that women seem to find so attractive. Chase was half Mexican and half we don't know and he really was a handsome man, if I can say that without anyone thinking something that isn't true about me. Anyway, he only had eyes for his wife. He was the guy that had two drinks and then drank water or soda the rest of the night. Don't get me wrong, he could cut it up with the rest of us, but when he said "no" he meant it and his wife and family were not on the menu for jokes of any kind and when she called, he went home. Chase was the quintessential perfect man that women talk about. Some of you may be asking yourself, how can that be so, how can a sniper, a killer of men, be the perfect man? That is something that you are going to have to sort out for yourselves, or maybe you could just accept that a man's profession is not necessarily his identity. It could just be his job.

Chase's partner in the field was Pat. Now Pat was kind of the opposite of Chase. Like Bryce, the Captain, Pat was a womanizer. He had a girl or four in every town we visited. He had no preference or type, he just liked women. He was not all hung up on booze as you might think. Don't get me wrong, Pat could tie one on when the occasion called for it, but for him the call did not come in as often as with some of the other guys. Also like his partner, Pat was devilishly handsome. But unlike Chase, Pat was the one that kept up with the latest trendy hairstyles, as best he could with the haircut regulations and when out of uniform, he kind of looked like a thug. Tattoos covered the vast majority of his body, including his butt cheeks. Before you ask, yes, he showed them off to whoever would look. On one butt cheek he had a cheeseburger with a local fast-food restaurant name from his hometown. Every time that he went home, all he had to do was drop his pants at the place to get a free meal. I never really understood it, it seemed like a lot of work to get a free burger. But it takes all kinds.

Who was I in this group? Well, I was the smartass who just happened to read regulations for fun. If ever there was a question about what the regs said about any given situation, they asked me. I had never gotten out of my training as a child, to read everything and commit as much of it as I could to memory and to cross reference things, so it all made sense in my head. After basic, I found that I rather liked maps and land navigation, so I added that to my must-know reading and any time I came to a different place, whether it was a new city or a new spot of sand, I got out the maps and got myself acquainted with the topography. Being with me meant that you never got lost physically speaking. My relationship with Doug was like Dean Martin and Jerry Lewis, I was his straight man that played into every idiotic thing that came out of his mouth. Sometimes, when he went just that one hair too far, I would just close my eyes and shake my head. I had nothing when he did that. This kind of made me the follower to his leader. It did not work that way in the field, but in social gatherings it definitely worked that way. That's how I got second fiddle with Patti, well that and I was terrified to speak to her. I have asked myself a thousand times, "What do you say to a goddess when you first meet her?" The answer is always, "hello." And yet, I could not even say that.

That was our team when Doug was courting Patti. They were quite the group of men and I loved them all.

———

It's interesting to remember those guys now as I lie here waiting for the final shot of my career. They were good men, one and all. I am no longer an enlisted man, now I am a light Colonel, and I asked for this mission. I am pretty sure that my shrink would have a reason why and I don't care if she does. I know why. I needed one last shot, one last successful mission and more than that, I needed this time of quiet, of peace where my thoughts are my own and no one needs me to do anything for them, except squeeze this trigger at the right time and aim true. I know why I am reflecting on these men and these moments, because without them all, I would not be the same man today, hell I may not even be lying on this berm. Without those men, I would probably be in a pine box feeding the worms. Without these events, I would not have had the courage or reason to stay in the Army for this long and without Patti and the children, I would not have had the direction or encouragement to make any of this happen. I know why I am here and why I am remembering these people and events. I don't need a shrink to tell me that.

I feel my mouth smile at the memories. I take in a small cleansing breath and focus on the site. There is nothing but empty roadway. My partner can sense my mood and shifts slightly.

My mind shifts to a wedding. Not my own wedding to Patti, but Doug's wedding to Patti.

6

The Gauntlet

Patti had to have it all. She was the daughter of a two-star general after all. It did not matter that Doug was just an enlisted man, and not a very high-ranking one at that. She had appearances to keep up and her parents would not have it any other way. I actually felt sorry for Doug, while still being envious.

Doug was still one of my best friends and a man I could count on to have my back. In truth, I may not even be alive had it not been for Doug. Hmmm... Maybe I shouldn't just drop a comment like that without telling the story.

It was during that sandbox mission that went sideways, right after the infamous Christmas Party. We were hopping sand dunes, looking for an insurgent compound that never stayed in one place more than a week or so at a time. Our unit had split the desert into a grid pattern, split up into twos and headed out to find the bad guys. So, you are probably wondering why we didn't just use a satellite to find these idiots, well that would have been just dandy, had satellites been that dependable at the time, which they were not... and for all you "why didn't you just" people who think that it was just a matter of flying a drone over the area to spot our targets well, drones have not been around that long and they were not all that dependable in the early days and guess what, the bad guy knows how to shoot shit down too. Real life is not a video game or a Hollywood movie. The good guys do not infiltrate a foreign country or hostile territory with impunity and just for the record, no plan, regardless of how precisely organized goes according to the plan after first contact because nobody has any idea exactly how the opposition is going to react to your plan. So please get over yourselves and stop Monday morning quarterbacking people who have actually done the job. Anyway, stop interrupting, and let me get back to the story.

The going was slow. We did not want to race over the dunes like some drunken kids on a California beach. We needed to crawl over the dunes and spot the top of each one before we reached it. It would not do to fly over a dune right into a nest of assholes with guns. And we had to do it with minimal light, because we all know that the only light in the middle of a desert at night is the moon. Headlights can be spotted miles away. But so can insurgent camps if you let them shine on their own.

Our biggest problem was that we could not really make the Humvees quiet. Sound travels across the desert like ice skates on smooth ice. Consequently, it was not really that big of a surprise when we came under fire.

When bullets are bouncing off of everything around you, your mind retreats to its safe zone. Then, it is up to your training. If you have been trained well, and if you have retained that training, then you have a better than average chance of getting out alive, because when your mind runs away, all you have left is your instinct and what you have trained your body to do. You will react. It is a fact. You will react, either with positive lifesaving action or with negative life-surrendering action.

What did we do? We were in a gauntlet, so we had to get out. I spun the Humvee in a circle and headed back out. Doug got on the radio and relayed our coordinates and our situation. Then, we shot back.

Of course, all of that happened in split seconds.

They had closed the gap behind us. So, we were in the center of about twenty guys with semi-auto rifles. Now, a military Humvee is somewhat bullet resistant. It is made of steel and bullets are made of lead. One is much stronger than the other. But, when you throw copious amounts of lead at anything, it will eventually penetrate. Glass, of course, regardless of how thick it is, does not take nearly as much lead pounding as the metal frame it is in.

It seemed like the windows and the windshield all shattered at once. They are all made of tempered glass, which means they do not shatter in sharp shards, but the little squared glass pellets are sharp enough to cut, and when they are travelling at any great rate of speed it only increases their chances of shredding flesh.

In less than five seconds, Doug and I were completely covered in glass. Lucky for us, very little of our skin was actually showing. I got a few scratches on my cheek and Doug got the same. We did not even register them at the time. What we did register is the fact that now there was no barrier at all between us and the fast-moving lead.

Please understand, this was not our first mission together, but it was the first time that Doug and I were alone in the shit together. You don't really know what your teammate is capable of, until you're in a situation like this one. We had respect for each other, sure, we had trained together and been through a lot of stuff together, even been deployed together several times. Doug Shelby was my brother. He was a man who I would trust my life with, and he felt the same about me, and now here in the sand-blasted armpit of the world, we both got the chance to prove to each other just how much we wanted ourselves and each other to live. Let me tell you, that was a life-altering experience.

Doug is an excellent shot, even from a moving vehicle, and I was keeping the truck moving, while shooting wildly with my pistol. Finally, after the longest twenty or thirty seconds of my life, Doug drops a couple of guys at about eleven o'clock, and I ram the truck towards the opening he had created in their line in the hopes that I can jam it through and get out.

Now, I know what you are thinking. Why did we not just point the truck in a direction and run the bastards over? The answer is simple; that is idiotic Hollywood crap. Nobody in their right mind drives a vehicle directly into semi-automatic gunfire. Not only would you be presenting two of the Humvees weakest spots, the radiator grill, and the front windshield, which we no longer had, to the enemy, but if either of those spots are compromised before you run the bad guy over, a third and arguably more vitally important weak spot will not only be exposed to gunfire, but probably exterminated, and rightly so, for being such a dumbass in the first place. That third thing is the driver in case you missed the metaphor. It can be done, as a last resort, but we were not there, yet.

So, there we were, driving hellbent for leather towards a small gap in the bad guys. Doug is reloading, again, and I am trying to drive and take aim with my handgun at the same time. Then, off to my left, at my ten o'clock, there was a guy. He had that rifle of his pointed right at me. We looked into each other's eyes. I do not know what he saw in mine, but I saw determination and a hint of victory in his. He had me dead to rights.

I fired my pistol at him. It was a wild shot. I just pointed my finger at him and squeezed the trigger. I saw the muzzle flash from his rifle. I saw him fall. For a tiny moment of time, I felt elation. I got him, but then I realize that although we were now through the gap created by Doug, my vision was getting dark. I could hear Doug yelling through a thousand gallons of water. We were still moving but I could not feel the steering wheel. My hands, both the one holding my gun and the one holding the steering wheel were growing cold. A sick cold nausea feeling was creeping into my insides. Something was terribly wrong, but I had no idea what it was. The only warm spot on my body was my neck and the warmth was growing. It began to burn and then... there was nothing.

I woke up six days later in a field hospital somewhere in Saudi Arabia. They tell me that the round went cleanly through my neck. It touched nothing vital, not my arteries and not my spine. How it did that, I have no idea. But I woke up to Doug grinning like a stuck pig in my face. "There you are! Welcome back to the land of the living, you son of a bitch!" He did look very pleased to see me. I, on the other hand, was feeling too bewildered and in too much pain to be very pleased with anything. I tried to say, "Hey, how's it going, fucker?" but it came out as nothing but a low hiss.

"Don't try to talk, dumbass. You got your throat shot. It was a damn lucky shot, but your neck still looks like a fat sausage."

I reached up to touch my throat and felt only bandages. I looked at Doug and hissed out a "What?"

"I was here when the nurse changed your dressing 'bout an hour ago. How that round missed anything important, I have no idea. But then again, the only really important thing dangles between your legs, right?" He chuckled at his own joke.

I smiled, I think, and tried to talk again.

"Hey, stop, really. They had to do some delicate surgery on your vocal cords. You will not be talking anytime soon and if you do, you might damage something that they cannot fix. So, zip it. Don't worry, I can talk for you." He grinned evilly.

Doug told me what happened after we had cleared the gauntlet. He had ripped my pistol from my hand and pulled the Shemagh from around his neck and folded it around mine. Then, he took both my hands and told me to hold it in place. He put them where they needed to be to staunch the bleeding. I could not feel my legs, but apparently my training had kicked in and my foot, the one that I could not feel, just held steady on the gas. Doug steered. He had already called for help, so it was not long before I was evac-ed out.

"Now you know the long and short of it. I'm gonna go find a tall one and try to get someone back home on the phone."

I smiled. At the thought of him calling Patti, I wanted to grimace, but I smiled anyway. I am not sure if my face was listening to me, but I did try.

"Don't worry brother, I'll let everyone know that you are thinking of them." And with that, Doug left so I could sleep.

Like I said, I do not remember anything after being shot. What I know is that Doug and my training saved my life that night. I am here because of him. So, when he asked me to be his best man, I jumped at the chance. The son of a bitch was marrying the woman of my dreams, and I was going to wish him well and celebrate his good fortune with him. Life is a bitch, isn't it?

Doug visited me regularly while I was in the hospital and stayed at my side when they released me. He never let me talk, but then again, I didn't really need to. He knew me well enough. He cracked jokes and made fun of me with the guys, as usual. I just smiled and nodded or used my facial expressions to speak for me. It was strange, but it worked.

One day, after getting my dressing changed again, I must have been looking a bit too serious for Doug. He sat me down and started talking. I am still not sure if it was for me or him.

"You got that bastard by the way. Did you know? You got him, the one who shot you."

I nodded because I did remember him going down.

"Don't feel guilty. I know you, you're always wondering who might be waiting for them. But it doesn't matter, right? We all picked these up." He patted the rifle that lay on his chest. "We all chose to play this game. All of us, them, and us. We all chose, and we knew the stakes and the possible consequences. Death has always been in the cards. You trumped him and you survived, and he didn't. That's not anyone's fault except his. He didn't have to pick up that gun and join the game. He could have stayed at home with whoever, but he didn't. He was in that sand, shooting at us. You shot true; he didn't. That's all there is. Okay?"

I nodded again. I knew that he was right. Still, it is hard to swallow, and it never gets easier. I like to think that you become immune to death, but you don't. You just learn how to hide what you are thinking.

———

It started snowing again. Off and on, that's how it is going to be with this snow. I can hear the snowflakes landing on branches. How is it that snowfall makes the world go so silent that you can hear the flakes land?

7

Their Wedding

Back to the wedding. I was the best man, so of course, I threw Doug the wildest bachelor party I could imagine. We had every cliché, kegs of beer, a live heavy metal band, mountains of food and of course, a stripper coming out of a cake and an after party in an expensive hotel room. It was a monumental party and Doug loved every moment of it, and so did I if I want to tell the truth.

The next morning was a different matter. There comes a time in every man's life when he realizes that no matter how much water you drink or food you eat, if you drink too much beer and whiskey, you will have a massive hangover the next day and you will most likely puke on something important or hard to clean. Doug and I had come to that conclusion at least a year before, but that did not stop us from making the same mistake again at the bachelor party. We both awoke in a puddle of puke with hangovers that would floor an elephant.

The good news was that we had a full three hours to clean up our act and look presentable for the wedding. The bad news was that we would pay extra for the hotel room that we had destroyed. We would ask ourselves for years how, and who, had managed to get puke on the drapes, eight feet off of the floor. No one ever copped to it. It had probably been the culmination of a bet that no one remembered.

We both thanked God that we had been smart enough to leave our tuxes with his mother. God only knows what might have happened to them had we not. We had also set aside a clean set of clothes at the hotel, where none of our brothers could find them, thank God, or they might have become part of some forgotten bet as well. We cleaned up and headed for Doug's mom's house and diligently hoped that we did not get pulled over. We knew that we would not have passed any sobriety test, let alone anyone's sense of smell. Good Lord, we stunk! It was so bad that we drove with all the windows down just so we would not puke... again.

Just shy of three hours later, Doug and I both stood at the front of the church. We still stunk, and we knew it. The odor of alcohol wafted off of us like the stench of a skunk. No amount of cologne could cover it. But we tried anyway. I think that we actually made it worse. Thank God we stood at least three feet from the first row. Not that I am certain it helped much. It wasn't just me and Doug. The entire team was standing in a wobbly stinky row right beside us. We were all clean and looked presentable, the pictures would be great. But real life was a stinky mess. And yes, we were all immensely proud of ourselves. Even Chase had exceeded his usual alcohol boundaries. He actually had drunk five shots and a beer. Then his wife had come and taken him home. His punishment for leaving the party early was that today, he had to smell all of us. Of course, we put him in the middle of the lineup. I actually saw him swallow his bile once or twice. Yeah, we smelled that bad.

When the music started, we all turned. Patti was a vision. No woman had ever looked so magnificent, so pure, and so sublime. I was in love all over again, and once again I felt envy and a bit of anger towards my best friend. He had won the prize of a lifetime. I wished them all the love and happiness in the world. I never wished anything else for them. But, sometimes, when no one else was around and I was feeling sorry for myself, I wished that it had been me that Patti had chosen. I never wished to be Doug, I wished that she had chosen me. After making that wish, I always chided myself, for her to choose me, I would have had to actually talk to the woman. And that is when I would pour myself a drink, and sometimes, I would actually drink it and on those days, I would drown myself in it.

The wedding was a whirlwind and over before I knew it. Patti was gone, completely out of reach for the rest of my life. I took it well. I grabbed a bottle of Johnny Walker and found a corner and this was one of those times that I drank it, all of it. I went home with someone. I do not remember ever getting her name.

—————

It is still snowing. It has turned into wet snow. I have worn my Gortex. I will be fine. My girl Mary will need some love when I get in. She is a vision. She has a long slim profile, beginning with a clean, lightweight 24-inch barrel with a sexy white dot front sight. Adding the front site is a personal choice. A rifle just doesn't feel like a rifle without iron sites. Mary is an M2010, and she is all mine. She uses a better 7.62 round than her predecessor, the M24, which I did not own, and she can hit a target at 1300 yards. I got Mary on my own, but the Army agreed with me... well we, snipers that is, and started issuing M2010's a few years ago. I will retire before they upgrade again and when I retire, Mary is coming home with me. This is her last shot at a human target, probably her last shot at a living target. Using Mary to hunt animal game, is not fair. But to use her to hunt human scum, well fairness has nothing to do with that.

I reach to the side of Mary's barrel and clump some snow together and put it in my mouth. No, I am not thirsty, cooling my mouth down will better hide my breath.

8

The Aussie Flight

Our first deployment after the wedding was fairly tame. We were not sent in to be snipers, although if the need presented itself, we would have certainly obliged. It did not. We spent our time going out on daily excursions into the surrounding countryside from our tent city base.

First off, you need to understand that not all bases where US servicemen are deployed are created equal. Military bases in the United States, and even those in many other countries where we are allied with the ruling government, are generally really nice and not under constant fire. This cannot be said for bases that are not in friendly countries. It is really not true for Forward Operating Bases or FOBs. These are the bases from which we plan and execute offensives into hostile territory. FOBs are usually located within a few miles of an enemy line. That is why they are called "Forward" Operating Bases. If we get deployed to an FOB, we are definitely not going to tell anyone prior to leaving and when we get there, any communication with our loved ones will not divulge our location or what we are doing.

Benghazi for example, was a base that was literally in the middle of hostile territory. There was no buffer zone between our people and the bad guys, except the walls that surrounded the Embassy, and that turned out to not work very well in the end. To be fair, those that were defending that Embassy when the shit hit the proverbial fan have nothing to be ashamed of, they fought harder and better than most folks will ever know. In the end, they were simply outnumbered and had no help from our beloved government.

The Embassy in Benghazi was also a bit of a rare item, in that they had actual brick walls that separated them from the bad guys. Most Joint Operation Bases that are on foreign soil are a collection of old brick or even mud brick buildings, a few trailers, and a whole lot of tents. Think M.A.S.H. I am sure that most people have at least seen a picture or two. Once you have the concept of tents in mind, now change those nice uniform, clean Army green tents to yellow and white striped circus tents with dirt floors, fill them with swarms of flies and surround them with mountains of trash. Now you are getting the picture. By the way, most Middle Eastern countries burn their trash at the end of each day, filling the air with a stench that lingers and seems to penetrate every pore of everyone and everything. The natives then look at the smoke-filled horizon and say, "Is not that sunset beautiful?" The sun is an angry-looking red globe set against a grey and black background. This experience helped me to decide to never live in a city where the sun or the sky is ever that color.

Speaking of the trash burning, the smoke damages the lungs and throats of everyone. The doctors have a new name for the "syndrome" that vets get from inhaling all of the myriad chemicals that are burned in that trash, they call it Afghanistan Agent Orange Syndrome. Vets who had to endure that crap get to spend the rest of their lives clearing their throats and many die of some kind of COPD, don't ask me to give you the full translation of the letters, it's the disease that eats the lungs and fills them with fluid so you can't process oxygen. Essentially, you drown without the benefit of being in any water. I have a friend, a former Navy Seal who came down with this shit. His internal organs, all of them started to melt. He was coughing up blood from his lungs and puking it from his stomach. He dropped from 210 pounds to 150 in a matter of weeks. We thought he had cancer, but no, he had this syndrome and would be dead in a matter of a month or so. The doctors scrambled trying to figure out what was wrong. Clearly, it was chemical poisoning, but which chemical? They had to backtrack and figure out where he was during all of his deployments to figure out which chemicals he had been exposed to, to kind of narrow down what was killing him. It turned out that it was the trash and all the chemicals in those piles of garbage that had invaded his body. Now once a day he takes a huge horse pill that is so big, he has to coat it with Vaseline to get it down. Yes, he knows that Vaseline is bad for you, but at this point, what is one more chemical? It has stabilized him. There is no cure. So, thank you sandbox and burning trash!

Anyway... We were sent to a place like that in Fallujah. Every day, we went out from the relative safety of that shit hole to get shot at by everyone outside the fence. We shot back, of course, and when we were out of ammo, we were done for the day. Mind you, we did not take just a few rounds of ammo, we took cans full of ammo... every day. It was not a pleasant job, but it was the job that they gave us, so we did it.

We all tried very hard after that deployment to forget what we had seen and what we had done. I am still working on that little task myself and my shrink is not too happy with my lack of progress. I will tell you about that shrink a little later.

Anyway, after going out and shooting people all day, we would come in, clean up in the mud floor showers and go to get some chow. The chow hall was an old single-wide trailer that had probably been a piece of shit in 1980, now it was a bigger piece of shit and it stunk. We were never quite sure if it was the trash outside or the cooking inside that made it stink, probably both. The cooks were some "friendly" Iraqis who would not know how to cook a decent meal if their lives depended on it. For my first breakfast on site, I asked for a fried egg, a slice of some kind of cooked meat and some toast. The cook promptly cracked 2 eggs and dropped them into the deep fryer. Then he sliced a slab of what looked like Spam but most definitely was not and threw it in on top of the disintegrated egg. When he figured this concoction was cooked, he poured it out onto a day-old piece of flatbread and handed it to me with a big smile. It looked and smelled disgusting. I tried drowning it in Tabasco sauce and ketchup and ended up eating most of it, much to my dismay as an hour later I was running for the latrine.

Needless to say, I was a bit weary of the food after that encounter and stuck to my MRE's as much as possible. That did not stop me from encouraging others to partake, for my amusement of course. One youngster, still in diapers, a true FNG (Fucking New Guy) came to town. He was craving some food from home, so I suggested the local pizza. How can you screw up pizza... right? Ha ha, well let me tell you, that ole boy behind the counter had never seen a pizza in real life and only had a picture to tell him how to make it. So, out came the flatbread, then came the ketchup and the goat cheese, because all cheese is goat cheese, then came the slices of that undetermined meat that came out of that sketchy looking tin and then it was topped with black olives... whole black olives, pits, and all. Well, that youngster must have had a stomach made of almost cast iron. It took nearly four hours before he got up in his skivvies and sprinted for the latrine. The most foul-smelling shit was oozing down his leg as he ran with his thumb shoved into his butt trying to hold it off. Half the camp could hear him howling as his bowels cut loose. I fell out of my bunk. I was laughing so hard that I thought that I could not laugh anymore, until that FNG came back through the tent door dripping wet from the showers and holding a dirty moth-eaten washcloth over his privates. He had apparently destroyed his tighty whities on the way to the latrine and had discarded them down the hole with everything else. I absolutely could not breathe, and I was not the only one. Welcome to the party at the ass end of the world!

The best part of all of that is that when it was that youngster's turn to be the veteran food connoisseur, he got the next FNG to eat the pizza. I fell out of my bunk again. Some of you might think that was cruel. Okay, you go to Fallujah, Benghazi, or some other random piece of dirt, get shot at every day, shoot back, and kill God only knows how many people and let's see how you let off steam by not doing something really stupid. Go ahead, I dare you. Encouraging others to eat bowel-cleansing pizza was tame and incredibly funny!

Nearly every night, after we had been out all day, we would come in and clean up and get some chow... I said that already, right? Well, most nights we could hear rockets soaring overhead and sometimes they would land close. So, what are you supposed to do when you're sitting in a trailer in the middle of a dirt pile and eating cottage cheese, yup made from goat milk, and been sitting in the sun for about eight hours before they bothered bringing it in to serve... where's the Tabasco... where was I... oh yeah... what do you do when you hear a rocket soar low over the trailer and explode in the middle of the tent city beyond? Well... I asked for more cottage cheese and Doug handed me the Tabasco. Together I, along with the rest of our team, ate and listened to the chaos on the other side of the trailer wall. What? Did you think that we ran out of the crappy trailer and made targets of ourselves? What are we going to do against a rocket launcher? We cannot even see the stinking sand lizards that are lobbing the rockets into the camp. But they sure as shit could have seen us if we had dropped our food, using the term "food" loosely, and ran out to engage a rocket launcher with a rifle. How stupid do you think that we are? Do not answer that!

Okay, so now you think that sitting in the crappy trailer makes us sitting ducks. On one hand you are correct, but until we confirm to the enemy where we are at, those idiots have no idea where the ducks are located. So, they are just lobbing rockets into our camp the same way that a bird hunter lobs a rock into a bush to try and flush the enemy into the open, so he can shoot them! In effect, we sit there and eat our goat cottage cheese with Tabasco until the shelling stops. We have an anti-rocket/missile gun that some brainiac took off of a ship, yup a ship and hauled it into the middle of the desert and set it up in the camp. The damn thing worked pretty good, so we got another one. Let those things do their job while I try not to get some more indigestion.

That deployment lasted for almost a year, just eighteen days shy to be exact. Now some deployments end with us going to Stuttgart, Germany to unwind for a couple of weeks before heading home. Those are some sweet times coming into Germany and enjoying the food, that does not make you run to the latrine and drinking the beer that is so thick you can cut it with a knife. Yup, Germany is a sweet stopping place. They have American fast food too, and if you order pizza, it is made the way that they make it in the good old US of A. No goat cheese here... unless you actually want it. I personally, do not want to have goat cheese ever again. Strangely enough, some Mexican dishes are made with goat cheese, but that food is actually edible.

We did not go to Germany after this particular deployment. We caught a ride on an Aussie plane with some of their guys coming in from some other tent city. I remember getting onto the plane and thinking "Good, at least they have seats in this tin can." I sat down and do not really remember much else until the cabin pressure changed just before landing. So, I was a bit groggy when I stumbled out of the plane with my crew and theirs. We all funneled onto a big bus. I had no idea where we were and I remember asking, it was more of a mumble, "Where the hell are we?" I did not get an answer that I could understand. I was too tired to decipher Aussie talk. I think that they were all drunk anyway.

I had found a seat next to Chase. The seat was really too comfortable, and the view was for shit. The backs of the chairs were too tall for me to see anything in front of me and it would not have done me any good anyway, it was nighttime wherever we were. So, I drifted off to sleep again and I am certain that I was not the only one.

I woke up again when Chase nudged me and said, "We're here, man." I asked him, "Where?" and he just shrugged and motioned for me to get moving. So I did. We all stumbled out onto a dock. Yes, a boat dock. We were all very confused. No one had any clue what country we were in, let alone why we were on a boat dock in said country. The Aussie guys all seemed quite pleased that we had "made it," to where and why did not seem to be something that they could answer with much clarity, until Dusty put on his big boy pants and demanded an answer that everyone could understand. "The Maldives, of course."

What? We were in the Maldives? Why... okay, so... what? We had never been shipped back home through the Maldives, so we were all very out of our comfort zone. The Aussies found our discomfort quite amusing and loudly led the way toward a row of yachts and small daily cruise ships. They kept saying, "Relax, you'll love this!" All I kept thinking was, what the hell did we get ourselves into this time? But, what the hell, let's do this!

We got onto a cruise boat and cast off into the dark. Now if you have never been on the water at night, you have never really lived. I have seen dark before, many times, mostly in the sandbox where there are few cities and a lot of nothing, but dark on the water, especially something other than a lake, is a different thing altogether. You find yourself staring at a fixed point in the sky, pick a star, any star and let yourself feel the motion of the boat, hear the water slapping an irregular pattern on the bow as the boat cuts through the water, in the background, listen to the low drone of men talking. Loud raucous voices seem very inappropriate out here, so even in their drunken state, the Aussies had toned it down a great deal. Even their laughter was muffled. The boat engine purred steadily, the boat bounced off of the tiny waves, the water slapped, and the world was at peace. It was such an overwhelming feeling. I felt like I could breathe and allow myself to truly relax. I felt safe.

Normally, when we come in out of the field, they take us to places that seem familiar, but aren't quite home. Places like Germany, England, and my personal favorite, Ireland. All of these places speak English. Now that sounds incredibly racist or something, but the fact is, everyone wants to be understood and to understand what someone else is saying. That is incredibly difficult when you are surrounded by people who either do not or refuse to speak a language that you understand. You have no idea what they are saying or plotting. So, you get paranoid. I mean, who wouldn't? You get shot at regularly, bombed constantly and you have no idea who is the good guy or the bad guy because they all dress the same, there are very few actual uniforms in the sandbox, and you can only trust about ten percent of those to be actual uniforms and not costumes. So, when you leave, you need to readjust to what you perceive to be normal. Normal for me includes people who at least try to speak a language that I can understand, food that doesn't create mass exodus in my stomach, green grass, and trees and oh yeah, the sound of running water. All of that and not fearing for my life every second of every day.

Saying that makes me realize that, it was the sound of the water that made me feel safe. In the sandbox, they have water, of course they do, but not in great quantities. They do have water collection pools... huh? Water collection pools look a lot like big depressions in the sand that are rectangular in shape and somehow fill up with water. The engineering is out of my wheelhouse. All I know about those things is that if you are driving through the desert and go over a dune too fast, you may end up nose-first in one of those bloody reclamation pools. We had to fish out more than one FNG that fell into one.

Anyway, the sky was changing. Soon the sun would crest the horizon and illuminate the world and I couldn't help myself, I smiled. I must not have been the only one, because the Aussies took that moment to notice their American buddies grinning like stuck pigs. "I guess you all liked our little surprise." I guess we did.

The resort sat above the water on a gentle rolling slope in a forest of olive, oak and fig trees and the bushes all seemed to have some kind of purple flower. It smelled wonderful, even from the boat. We docked and piled out. Now was the time that the Aussies chose to explain what the Sam Hill was going on. Apparently, the owner of this resort, a place that rich folks paid about ten grand a week to enjoy, was the best friend of one of these Aussie blokes. So, every time his unit returned from a deployment, they come to Malta for a couple of weeks R and R. We really picked the right bunch of guys to make friends with this time around!

The inside of the resort made us Americans dumbstruck. We met the owner, and the help took us to our rooms. We had a suite with four bedrooms and a giant and, I do emphasize the word "giant" living area right in the middle. The Aussies got the same across the hall. The view, the smell, the colors... all of it was amazing! I looked for a short time, we all did. Then one by one we all wandered off to our rooms and about three days later we all woke up and wandered back out. When it's time to rack out, it's time to rack out. We felt safe so, we slept. We only woke up when we did because the damn Aussies brought us some food and were making such a fuss that we couldn't get back to sleep.

A hot meal and a hot shower later, we were all headed for the little shopping area where we could get some swimwear. None of us had packed anything that could be considered swimwear, so we shopped. There we were in a tiny little shopping area that was packed to the gills with stuff to buy and all they had were Speedos. Not just Speedos, but small and medium Speedos. What the hell man! We had just spent the better part of a year doing nothing but hunting insurgents and working out in the gym. We had all put on some muscle. I was up to about 220 and you are not going to get that much poundage into a small or medium-sized Speedo without a shoehorn.

I got the biggest pair they had and still felt like the cartoon guy on the Duluth underwear commercial. But I was not daunted. If I was going to be showing my family jewels to everyone at the resort, then I was going to do it garishly! I bought the silky-looking American flag Speedos and stuffed myself into them. And that, ladies and gentlemen, is when I understood some men's desire to man-scape. I had hair sticking out every which way but when I saw some of my team, and let's face it, you gotta look even when you're not supposed to... some of the guys needed hedge clippers. I mean yeah, we had seen each other in the altogether before, but again, you are not supposed to look, that's just creepy. But right now, with everyone in Speedos... well it was impossible. Most of all, for me it was Doug, my best buddy Doug with his thinning dusty red hair on the top, who knew that he would be bright red and furry from his chest through his belly button down to the tops of his Hobbit feet? I guess what they say is true, most Irishmen come from the Viking hordes! Now those guys are some hairy bastards and who knew, so was Doug!

So, an hour later, there we were, all eight of us, lined up like sheep outside of the local beauty salon waiting for our own wax job. Now, I am not going to say just how mentally unpleasant that whole affair was on the lot of us. To say that we were embarrassed would be a massive understatement. But damn it all, we were in the Army, and we needed shearing if we were going to be all that we could be in those tiny ass Speedos!

Here is another "who knew?" for you. Who knew that you could get sheered using hot wax or a razor or both? You know that at this point in my career I was a single man. I had not even been in a serious enough relationship to live with a woman, so color me shocked when the beautician gave me the choice. My mind wanted to steer away from the hot wax near my family jewels, but she assured me that the wax produced a better product. Huh? She explained that the skin down there is really sensitive... duh... no, really, it will get razor burn if you are not super careful and even then, it's a crap shoot. But the wax, if done correctly will not give you razor burn and the cleared area will stay clear for a longer amount of time. She guaranteed me that she was very gentle and knew what she was doing. Long story shortish, she talked me into the wax.

Here is the rub, you have to get out the man clippers before you can wax. These are the clippers that they use to shave your head in Basic, except smaller and with a lot of fancy attachments. I closed my eyes and grit my teeth and tried not to flinch when I felt the vibration of those clippers in my nether regions. This gave me a whole new appreciation and meaning for the word "'vibrator." I gotta tell you, having a complete stranger lifting and moving my junk around really felt odd, and no, it was not in any manner arousing!

Before I knew it, she was done with the clippers. I wanted to look, but was kinda afraid, so I did it anyway. It looked as odd as it had felt. My twig and berries were out and about, with no cover or camouflage. She had clipped all my light brown hair, from my pelvis down to my toes to a nice even snip. I am not nearly as hairy as Doug, but there was a considerable pile of fur on the floor. My family was many generations removed from their Irish and German roots and we had a healthy dollop of English blood in us, so hence, I was not a very hairy man... anyway, my hair had been trimmed down to the height of a number one, i.e., the first Basic haircut. I was just thinking that it did not look too bad when I saw the lady approaching with a steaming bowl, some cloth like strips and a short pizza flipping spatula. I got nervous all over again!

The wax was not hot, it was pretty warm, warm enough to be uncomfortable in some areas, but not so much so that I was screaming in pain... until she let a strip cool and ripped it off! I came up like I had been goosed and nearly backhanded the woman who was bent over my nethers. Then I saw it, a long red welt forming on my upper thigh. Oh, dear Lord, what had I gotten myself into? I laid back with a heavy sigh and grunted when she asked if I wanted her to continue. What was I going to do, I couldn't stop when I was only partly done. I would look ridiculous. I swallowed my pain and clung to my pride as she applied and then rudely removed the strips of hot wax. About 45 minutes later, she declared me done. She had talked me into doing all of my legs, right down to my ankles. When I looked down, I looked like I had sat in a Jacuzzi for too long, but thank the Lord, she had left my jewels alone. They only got a haircut. My legs on the other hand... I suppose I could claim it was sunburn.

She gave me a jar of ointment for the waxed areas and told me to apply it several times in the next few hours and the redness would dissipate quickly. I guess it also had some topical pain killer in it. She rubbed it all over my legs and they instantly began to feel better. Okay, I figured that I could do this, after all, I had not seen the other guys yet. I was really hoping that someone was worse, so I could make fun of them, and they would forget about how funny I looked.

When we all got back to the resort, we compared shearings by modeling our Speedos for each other. My legs had gone down to a moderate color of pink, so I was actually feeling surprisingly good when I stepped out of the room that I shared with Doug into the common area. Doug was in the bathroom changing. The guys were in variant degrees of shorn. Apparently, Chase, took after his Salvadoran mother and had thick black hair everywhere. He had had to have his ass cheeks waxed. But this was not new for Chase, because he had so much hair on his ass, he had problems with ingrown hairs that got infected. He had needed surgery twice to get the cysts removed that were caused by the hairs. He had never had anything else waxed, and the lady had him in there for nearly two hours getting him trimmed up.

The thing that I found remarkable is that I could tell which guys had chosen to use a razor instead of wax. I could see the bumps forming at the edges of their Speedo. They had cream too. Hopefully, it worked as well on the razor burn as it did on the waxed skin. Finally, Doug emerged. He looked like he had lost a few pounds! And they had even waxed the tops of his toes and hands! Wow, he was a changed man! We had a good laugh and drank some local brew with a hearty dinner. The next day we were going to wear our Speedos and prance in the crystal-clear water and play in the sand.

The next day dawned. We all headed out in the general direction of the water. We were definitely self-conscious at first. But then we noticed that we were attracting a lot of attractive female attention and that is when we became buffoons. Each of us trying to outdo the other in some kind of competition to get the most attention. In the end, we all paired up, yes even the married men, although they did not carry it through to a sexual conclusion... well there was Jake.

And that, ladies and gentlemen was my one and only trip to the Maldives and my one and only time in a pair of Speedos that were too small, however, it was not the only time that I man-scaped. And that is all I am going to say about that.

I have been laying on this berm for a long time now. My legs are wanting to do something, so I tighten all of my muscles in one leg and hold it for 30 seconds then I release and tighten the other leg. I do this several times trying to get some circulation moving.

I cannot help but chuckle a little when I remember that shearing. The thing that I remember most clearly was not the actual act of being shorn, it was when the hair started growing back. I itched everywhere! I bet some of you can relate.

9

Ms. C. S. Cane

The Maldives was a great place to unwind and gather our thoughts, but unfortunately, that long stay in the sandbox brought up some sludge for nearly all of us. When we made it stateside, we were all debriefed and almost all of us ended up being assigned a shrink. Now you know that I have had a shrink off and on since I was fifteen, so meeting a new one was kind of old hat for me. At least I thought that it should be.

I went to the local veteran's hospital where most of the shrinks are housed. The parking garage smelled of piss and cigarettes, just like any city parking garage, it reminded me how much I hated the city. The hospital had been renovated and expanded recently so there was a lot of paint and carpet covering the old cracks and deteriorating plaster. Nothing could cover the old smell of blood, piss, medicine, fear, and death. Those things never leave an old hospital. I chose a new elevator, hoping to escape some of the smell. It let me out into a corridor that went left into the old wing, and right into the new wing. My doctor was in the new wing.

The carpet muffled my steps as I trudged towards his office, I was to see Doctor Cane in room 432. A couple of turns and I found the office and stepped in. The receptionist took my name and told me to have a seat.

I had not waited long before a slightly overweight middle-aged black woman came out of the doctor's office to greet me. "Hello, my name is C.S. Cane, you must be Corporal Harrington." She held out her hand. I took it and we shook. She invited me into her office and in the first few minutes of the usual small talk I was reminded of Ms. Geraldine. Like her, Mrs. Cane was a woman that had children of her own, a broken marriage, and had seen a few things in her life. Ms. Cane differed in that she had remarried twice before throwing in the towel. This left her kind and a bit gregarious while still having a no-nonsense approach to life and to her patients. There would be no bullshitting this woman, nor would she brook smartass or half-answers. She wanted the unvarnished, unashamed truth. Most of her intensity came from how she looked at you. Some people just have a look that tells you to "cut the shit and speak the truth."

Now, I admit my initial thought concerning Ms. Cane was, "What the hell is this middle-aged black woman going to do for me? We literally have nothing in common." She had never been in the military, she was a woman, and she was black. I could not see any common ground and I do not think I am being racist when I say that. I was a young military white man. I was perplexed. But, having had several shrinks already, I was kind of open to giving it a shot. I had little choice. I could have requested a different person, but I figured that I had been given one hell of a second chance by a little old lady that had no reason to help me and had nothing in common with me, so maybe this was just another one of those things that you just have to try.

During that first "session" where we just talked to get to know one another, I realized that I liked this woman's personality. I could speak to her, and she did not shrink from me, and believe me, I tried to shock her a few times. She just absorbed it and shot something back. So, the decision was made, maybe I could learn something from this woman, maybe she could help me.

In the second session, she asked me, "So, Steven, what's on your mind? What keeps you awake at night?"

I sat staring at her for a long minute or two. She stared back just waiting for an answer. She was patient. I was not certain how I could start, or if I even wanted to, but suddenly I just blurted out, and I surprised myself. "I have killed so many people." It came out almost as a whine.

"Isn't that your job?" Her tone was flat. It took me aback.

"Yes... no, not... not like that." My voice got quiet. I was embarrassed and angry. I had never noticed the anger before.

"Tell me, like... what, how?" She had no notepad, I was not laying down on a couch and her voice, her tone was conversational, like two friends just talking.

I, on the other hand, was wringing my hands while I stared at them. I could feel the anger building in me like a volcano. But I did not want to erupt. Why was I so angry? "I don't understand why I'm so angry right now." I looked up to catch her eyes. I could feel hot tears coming to mine and suddenly, I felt like my teenage self again and I wanted to run, but I held myself in my chair.

"Who are you angry at, yourself, someone else?" Her voice had changed. It was calm and caring.

What kind of question was that! Who am I angry at? How can I be angry at myself? But, again, unbidden, I said, "Both" and the admission was like a relief valve. The anger oozed out of me, and I felt deflated and disoriented. I started shaking my head.

"I joined the Army, to protect people and yet... there are just so many people that will never go home to their families, because of me." There I had said it.

"Why did you kill them?"

Why? I had never really thought of why, not back then anyway. This one question and the answering of it, eventually put me on an entirely different journey in life. But right now, confronted with it for the first time, it only fed my confusion. Because it confused me, my anger rose again, and I lashed out. "Why, you want to know why? I'll tell you, because those were my orders, that's why!" I raised my voice and leaned forward in an attempt to intimidate.

"Alright, you were ordered to kill all of those people that you now feel guilty about, does that sum it up?"

The intimidation clearly had not worked. But her question had hit home. I could say that I had been following orders, but my father would remind me of the Nazi defense at Nuremberg. They had just been following orders too. In the end, I had to come to the realization that I was the jackass who had followed those orders. I have to take responsibility for what I have done and in that, I have to come to terms with how that makes me feel and how that is going to affect the rest of my life.

"I guess it comes down to 'were they lawful orders'?" I said out loud, not really making the statement for Doctor Cane, really just trying to save face.

"Were they lawful?"

"Yes" I thought hard on every instance. We had done some horrific things, but we had done them to save lives. Yet, the faces that I see when I close my eyes would beg to differ with that account.

"It does not make you a bad man to kill one to save another, if that is what you did." She said in a matter-of-fact tone.

"When did we get the right to make that decision?" I growled.

"Do you want the legal version?"

"No, I want... I don't know what I want." I threw myself back in my chair. I felt like I was talking in circles.

"It sounds like you want absolution, but I am not allowed to broach the subject of religion and I am not qualified to absolve you."

I started shaking my head again, absolution, is that what I wanted, to be absolved of my sins? "I don't know Doctor, I don't know. Can we stop talking now? I have a lot to think about."

"Yes, we can stop talking, but I have some homework for you. I want you to sit down and write about the incident that bothers you the most and bring it back for the next session."

"What?" I am not a child. What the fuck?

"What part of the assignment was unclear?"

Well, I did not like it but, the assignment was perfectly clear. I thanked her for her time and left.

Over the next week, I tried a few times to start writing, but it would either turn into a breakdown and cry session or I would destroy a pen by jabbing it like a knife into the paper and screaming at the top of my lungs. I went through several of those legal pads and when the next session came up, I had nothing on paper to bring.

Ahh, there is movement at the other end of my scope. My spotter and I both dial in just a hair more and see that it is not our target. It is a local in an early 70s model pickup. The back of the truck looks and sounds like it is full of boxes of chickens. Neither of us relaxes until the truck is well past us and even the sound of it is no longer audible. We are pretty sure that the driver had not seen us. Still, it seems odd to the both of us. That truck had probably been an advanced scout for the man who is our target.

I am weary of thinking back on my sessions with Doctor Cane. Maybe I will come back to it later. My mind drifts to happy times with Doug and Patti.

10

Their First Child

When Doug and Patti had their first child, I was the man who drove her to the hospital, because Doug was too nervous to drive.

It was a bouncing baby boy. Doug named him after his father and hers, of course. His name, Michael Gabriel. He had Doug's dusty red hair and his mother's gentle manner and green eyes. I fell in love, again.

The boy is what really cemented Doug to his father-in-law. Up until then, there was still a lot of friction between them. Doug was still an enlisted man, in comparison to a two-star, he was nothing.

This newly found comradery with the General caused Doug to rethink his life and start prodding me with new ideas as well. It was because of this child, that Doug and I both went back to school. It was not easy, what with deployments and family, school was tough to fit in, but we managed it. We did a lot of online classes and took the same classes at the same time, so we could help each other. When it came to the math stuff, we both got tutors. We were lousy at math. Now, I have to add this, online classes back then are not what they are now. We had to log into a school portal to turn in our work and had a kind of call in once a week to participate in a group chat kind of over the phone and online at the same time. It was a monumental pain in the ass! But we got it done.

We both majored in Business Management. We figured that we would be youngish when we retired, young enough to start a business and be our own bosses. Our first thought was to open a bar. A bar that served specialty beers, maybe even we could make some of those beers ourselves. Patti saw it a different way and in no time flat, our micro-brewery bar became a restaurant with a bar. Then she added in her big caveat that our business needed to be family-friendly. Well, one look at their son, and the decision was solidified. We would open a family-friendly restaurant that served wine and beer and no bar at all. It was a decision that we were all very happy with.

I was around the family so much that Doug's son called me Uncle Steve. I liked it. Patti, on the other hand, saw no reason why Uncle Steve could not have an aunt attached to his arm. She set me up on more dates than I can count on two hands. I am not saying that I did not enjoy the company, but compared to Patti, every other woman was a poor copy. None of them could even light a candle to her. But I could not tell her that. Hell, I could not even speak to her that first night. That is how I got into this mess in the first place.

I went out with them all. Some of them even warranted multiple dates. One of them was good enough to actually convince me that I might get serious about her. But she ultimately did not feel the same.

It all became a kind of game between Patti and me. She would find a beautiful single woman and introduce us. I would size the lady up, take her out a few times, and discover that we were not compatible.

Patti was always undaunted. She seemed to take it as a personal challenge to find the perfect woman for me. All she really needed to do to find that woman was look in the mirror. I could not tell her that. She was my best friend's wife. She was the mother of his son. I would never speak that way to her or even hint to either of them of my feelings.

Oh, don't misunderstand, I was not the guy who lowered his head or deliberately lost eye contact with her, that would have been a sure giveaway. I acted, or so I thought, like I was talking to my best friend's wife. I treated her with respect, joked with her, I even had conversations with her that did not include Doug. But I never crossed a line. I never stared at her... at least I never got caught staring at her. I never acted inappropriately around her, and I never gave her reason to suspect my true feelings. At least, that is what I always thought, but she is a woman, and they always find out.

Meanwhile, we men, Doug, the General, and me, took great joy in teaching Michael in all things related to being a man. For his second birthday, he got toy cars, a cop uniform, an army uniform, and a toy gun and holster from the men in his life. Mom and Grandma Esperanza promptly removed the gun and gave him a plastic baseball bat and baseball. We could not argue with that, it was still a man thing and he got the guns back a few years later anyway because while we were playing catch with him and showing him how to bat a ball, we put out a window and well... Okay, it went something like this... Like I said, it was on Mikey's second birthday. He had half his presents confiscated and put on a shelf and unlike many that young,

Mikey noticed it. So, I suggested that us guys take Mikey to the park to throw a few around and just show Mikey the right end of the bat. But that is not what happened.

"Hell, we can just toss it around in the front yard. We don't need to go to the park." Doug piped in nixing the trip to the park. Mind you the park was about a block away. Doug and Patti lived in a nice suburban housing complex with wide streets and houses with nicely manicured front and back yards and sidewalks. Most of his neighbors parked their cars in the garage or in their driveways, so the streets were fairly clear most of the time. It was a nice neighborhood of middle-class homes. Doug and Patti's front yard had a nice lawn that was bordered by flowers of all types. The backyard was in an unfinished state. That's why neither of us suggested the backyard.

Anyway, the General and I agreed that the front yard would do as long as we kept a close watch on Mikey, to keep him out of the street.

It was slow going for all of us. The ball was only a small plastic one that stopped dead when it hit the thick grass. There was a lot of tapping the ball with the tiny plastic bat, watching the ball fly about a foot away from the bat and sink into the grass. Then Mikey had to navigate the grass with his little two-year old legs and find the ball. Suffice it to say, no one was having any fun. The General made an excuse to go into the house, Mikey was ready to follow him. But then Doug, in an attempt to keep his son's attention snagged a real baseball and bat out of the garage. That ball moved a little further from the bat but it also caught in the grass. After about 10 more minutes of this new torture and after the first 20 minutes with the plastic bat and ball both Mikey and Doug were showing signs of frustration.

Doug stopped. He looked up and down the street. There was nothing. "Hey, let's just go out into the street. That way at least I can lob a ball or two that Mikey can chase. Cuz this shit is boring." And without waiting for me to agree, he stepped into the street and beckoned his son to him.

We played for the better part of half an hour. Doug would hit the ball and I would pretend to race Mikey to retrieve it. But children are easily distracted and they get bored quickly. We lost him when a neighbor's automatic sprinkler came on and water started filling the gutter. He toddled over, plopped his diapered tail onto the sidewalk, took off his sandals and put his feet in the water. Doug shook his head and nodded to me. Then he threw me the ball. We played catch for several rounds but then, Doug picked up the bat again and hit the ball, lightly in my direction. I did not have a glove. I was not going to catch anything going too fast, but Doug did not seem to care about my stinging hands. His hits got increasingly harder and I was moving further away from him to get to them. Some I simply knocked down and let roll so I could retrieve them. I even asked for a glove. He just called me a "pussy" and hit another one.

This went on for about 15 minutes. Then I saw a look in his eye. I knew that the next ball that he hit was going to be hard and it was, it just didn't go the way he thought that it would. Just as he threw the ball into the air, Mikey let out a screech like a screaming Banshee, Doug jerked in mid swing. The bat connected, but not correctly. The ball sliced away from Doug and headed at an angle for his open front door.

Inside the house, Esperanza and Patti had both heard Mikey and were coming to investigate. The ball and Miss Esperanza both got to the door at the same time. The ball, like I said was at an odd angle, it struck the door, shattered most of the small window panes and ricocheted right into Miss Esperanza's face. Her nose exploded in a gush of blood and she and the ball dropped one on top of the other onto the floor. Both Esperanza and Patti screamed. Mikey, who had originally squealed because he had found a worm, had just stuffed said worm into his mouth and bit down when he heard his Mommy and Grammy scream, so like any other 2-year-old in the world under similar circumstances, he started to cry, loudly.

Meanwhile, Doug from his vantage point and me from mine could not see what had happened inside the house. I made a beeline for Mikey. He was crying and on the wrong side of the street. I scooped him up, pulled what was left of the worm from his mouth and headed for the house. His crying began abating once I picked him up and got the icky out of his mouth. Doug was headed for the house, where the women had screamed. He got there seconds before me.

Now we had both seen our share of blood, but when you see it coming from the face of a woman like Miss Esperanza, well I know that I was in a state of shock and panic. Well, as panicked as I could be by that time in my life. Doug meanwhile, dropped into medic mode. He was not a medic, but we all know the first thing to do is stop the bleeding. He rushed to the kitchen to get a towel. I handed Mikey off to Patti and knelt down to help Miss Esperanza to her feet and escorted her to the couch where she could lie down.

"Get some ice while you're there!" I yelled to Doug, who spun on his heel to retrieve ice while simultaneously tossing the towel to me.

Patti had dropped Mikey on the floor with a sippy cup of water and was now hovering over her mother. The General had been in the bathroom when this all had started. He had emerged to chaos. But like the General that he was, he went out and started a car, pulled it up to the doorway with the passenger side to the door and emerged barking orders.

106

I was wiping blood from Miss Esperanza's face. Her nose was broken, badly. Ice was not going to help at this point. I had seen the General pull up the car and I knew that there was only one thing that I could do for this woman.

"Move the coffee table!" I barked to anyone listening. I don't know who moved it but it was not in my way when I knelt down, scooped Miss Esperanza into my arms, and headed for the waiting car. Whoever had moved the table had read my mind, they had opened both car doors as well. I slid her into the back seat and put her head in her daughter's lap while the General climbed back into the driver's seat. I looked up at Patti's stricken face and said, "I'll take care of Mikey." I glanced at the front seat as I backed out and shut the doors and mouthed the word, "Go" and stepped back. The General wasted no time.

I found Doug standing in the middle of the living room holding a towel of ice and looking a lot like I imagine a man would look had he just been convicted of treason. "I broke my mother-in-law's face." He said quietly.

"Yes, you did."

"I am so fucked."

"Yes, you are."

I stayed and took care of Mikey, just as I said that I would. And to be honest, I was glad to have him to hide behind when the General and Patti walked back through that door. He had been very upset by the commotion, even if he did not understand it. So, I had changed him, bathed him and given him a sippy cup of warm apple juice to help him sleep. I was on the couch holding him when they walked back in. I saw the looks on their faces. It was a mixed bag of exhaustion, worry, acceptance, and anger.

"Where's Doug?" The General asked.

I jerked my head to indicate direction and said, "Back porch." The General started in that direction. "How is she?"

Patti had made her way to the couch. "She will be okay. They want to keep her for a few days for observation. She lost a lot of blood and they had to operate to remove bone slivers and reconstruct her sinus cavity." She reached for Mikey.

"I got him. You will wake him if you take him." Patti pulled back. I got up and took Mikey to bed.

When I came back out to the living room, I could hear the General giving Doug a piece of his mind. "What the hell were you thinking. boy? You were supposed to be playing with your son! Sometimes, you are the most inconsiderate, short-sighted, lame-brained idiot that I have ever seen! You are a father and a husband, grow up and start acting responsibly!"

There was more, a lot more, but I tuned it out. This was not my place. I saw Patti on the couch. She had been crying. I wanted to put my arm around her and comfort her, but that was not my place either. I just stood there, in front of her. "Can she have visitors?"

"Not tonight, but tomorrow."

"Good, I would like to apologize to her. I am so sorry, Patti. I should have stopped it."

"Stopped what? Stopped Doug from being a child? I don't think that you have that kind of power." Anger was seeping into her words.

"Still, I am sorry. If there is anything that I can do... for any of you." I let it hang in the air between us. I could hear Doug defending himself on the back porch. "Look, he's my son and I would like to raise him my way... without so much damn interference from you and your wife!" That outburst was impossible to tune out.

Patti looked up at me. There was clearly something on her mind. But it seemed that she could not bring herself to say it. "No, Steven you have nothing to be sorry for, thank you for taking care of my son." She left it open and lowered her head. An argument had broken out on the back porch and it was getting louder. Patti looked embarrassed.

"I should let you guys have some privacy. Maybe I'll see you at the hospital tomorrow." Patti nodded but did not look up. The General and Doug sounded very heated. It could come to blows. Should I stay and run interference? I could, but it would seem like I was taking sides, and right now, I am on the General's side. Doug had been irresponsible and someone had gotten badly hurt. What if someone had died? But he was my best friend. I couldn't take sides right now while tempers were flaring. "I should go. You guys have some things to work out."

Patti nodded but did not raise her head. I saw a teardrop hit her hand. I found the Kleenex box where it had landed in all the commotion and pulled one and handed it to her while depositing the box on the table in front of her. She started to take it from me and allowed her hand to linger close to mine. Then she smiled, and for all the world I was stunned. Her face was red and her eyes puffy. She had snot running from her nose, that she quickly wiped away, and yet she was the most beautiful thing that I had ever seen and all I wanted to do was hold her, comfort her and make everything that made her cry disappear. Instead, I smiled back and knelt down in front of her and used the proffered hanky to wipe her eyes. "Your mom will be okay. I'll make sure of it if I have to threaten a few Doctors' lives." I said it somewhat jokingly, and she giggled lightly in her throat while smiling bigger, if that is possible.

"Thank you, Steven. I don't know what I would do without you... you are such a great help." Halfway through her sentence she realized that as a married woman, she was much too close to me, and I to her. She changed what she had intended to say and broke eye contact. I got the hint. I gave her hand a squeeze as I passed off the damp hanky and stood up and turned towards the door. "Try to have a better night, and if you guys need anything at all, someone to watch Mikey while you visit your Mom or anything, let me know."

She smiled at me again and said, "Thank you. We will."

I went home and poured myself a tall boy of Whiskey. It was still sitting on the kitchen counter when I woke up the next morning. I poured it down the sink and headed for the hospital.

Of course, Miss Esperanza recovered, but she had acute sinus troubles and perpetual allergies after that incident. She also kept her distance from Doug. His comment about her meddling, had struck a chord with both her and the General. The General was a lot more critical of Doug and Miss Esperanza was seldom around when Doug was at home. As for Doug, he was extremely happy that his outburst had resulted in "that damn woman" not being around so much. He felt more like the "man of the house" because she wasn't there. I, for one, had no idea that he was in such competition with Patti's mother, and for the record, I missed her. But, then again, I was not married to Patti. I had no idea what life was like in that relationship.

Accidents and family drama aside, Michael was solidly growing, so Doug and Patti started trying for another child. For some reason they were not having any luck. They went to see a fertility doctor and found out that Patti had some kind of woman thing that was going wrong. They could get pregnant again, but it would be difficult, and the pregnancy would be hard on her. They decided that they wanted to try for one more and call it quits after that. Patti desperately wanted a girl.

The only thing good that came out of this trying time, was that Patti was so focused on their relationship and her ability to become pregnant that she stopped setting me up. Looking back, it may have been one of the loneliest times of my life. Even though Patti had been focused on finding me a woman, she had at least been somewhat focused on me. Now, her focus was entirely on Doug. Even their son was in the back seat for a time.

It was about this time when our rotation came up again. It was time to deploy again. Doug tried to get out of it. Unfortunately, the only way that he could get out of it is if he claimed personal hardship. Trying to get pregnant does not qualify as a personal hardship.

———

Snow is beginning to accumulate on my front iron site. I do not need it, the iron site that is. The site picture through the glass has not changed. The road ahead is clear. Funny that my target chose to use such a seldom-used road. He probably thought that with less traffic, there was less chance of danger. Boy was he wrong. That's okay, he'll never be this wrong ever again.

Thinking back on those early years with Doug and Patti, I seem to remember quite a few times when Doug was an ass to her and her family. Maybe it was just my perception at the time that kept me from seeing it. The snide comments, the way he often dismissed Patti's opinions and then there was the way that Miss Esperanza looked at Doug, even before the broken nose incident. Had I been so lost in my own problems that I completely missed what might have been happening inside of their family?

11

Not Expendable

You know when they talk about dogs having separation anxiety disorder? Well, that is how Doug was acting before he even left the house. When we got into country, the anxiety got worse.

We still had a job to do, and just when I thought Doug had his head on straight and in the game, he would say something that told me his mind was in the States, with Patti. I could not blame him. Despite everything, their marriage seemed to be on track, and they truly loved each other, much to my chagrin. Still, understanding or not, he was my partner and I needed him with me.

We were in country for six days before we were given our assignment. It was fairly simple but getting in place would be a bit tricky. We were to sit on a compound in the desert where, word had it, an Al Qaida big meeting was to take place. Our job would be to take out as many of these leaders as we could.

As you can imagine, with this kind of thing, their security would be ridiculous. We may get in, but the chances of getting out were worse than mine and Doug's escapade with the gauntlet. Still, we would never get a better chance to take out so many leaders. Why do we not just bomb the shit out of the compound, you ask, because some bleeding heart back home would have kittens if there was just one person in that compound who was not suspected of terrorism and who also managed to die in the blast. Forget the fact that every other one of the eighty or so people in there are responsible for hundreds, if not thousands, of deaths and thousands of more people enslaved. Those statistics do not matter to the assholes at home, no, they have to save one person and damn the rest. So, people like me and Doug and our unit get to go in and spend our blood to protect everyone else. We are proud to serve, do not get me wrong, but once in a while, it would be nice if our fellow American citizens did not consider us all expendable.

Now that whole tirade does sound just a bit like what Doctor Cane wanted on paper, hmmm... maybe I should have just spit it out the next time she asked me "Why?" And for the record, I apologize for my outburst. Sometimes, my anger gets the better of me. I am not angry at anyone in particular, but no one likes to be treated like shit, especially if they are doing something nice for someone, and I think that placing my life in danger to help complete strangers is a "nice" thing. So, please forgive me for my outburst.

For the record, I do not feel expendable. I feel like my life means more than that to someone, Doug, and Patti, and maybe even the General and his wife. My parents are gone, and my dear sister Katie went with them. I was fifteen when my whole life got turned upside down, well you all know the story. The point is that service is all that I have known since. Mrs. Hasse had seen potential in me, despite what I had done, and she believed that God had spared me for a reason. Now I know that a lot of people would wonder what kind of God saves a boy who becomes a sniper, I tell those people, He's the kind of God that is okay with spending one life to save many. In my mind, I tell myself that if He needs me to spend my own life to save many, then so be it.

Wow, that is almost exactly what I said was wrong with the bleeding hearts back home, spending my blood for strangers and all. It's okay if God wants that from me, but I am pretty not okay with some politician wanting that from me. It also sounded like I am ready to die. I suppose that I am, as much as anyone can be. At least I think so.

I am not saying that I want to die. Of course, I don't. Only psychos want to die. I am not that. I just know that God has a plan, and I fit into that plan somehow. I don't need to understand it or even my part in it, I just know that I am part of it. There are those that say, "What kind of God sanctions war?" Honestly, the kind that has enemies. Who could be an enemy to a God you ask... probably those that kill His people? Now, these people with their stupid questions are the ones that are complaisant with the murdering rag heads that have a religious... yup, that means their god is involved, jihad against infidel Christians. So, to sum it up, it's okay for them to force their religion on everyone, but it is not okay for Christians to complain about it.

But I digress. I was telling you a little more about my family. As you know my dad was an auto mechanic. He often traded fixing someone's car for food or something else he could fix up for us kids. He once traded a carburetor rebuild for two bikes that he turned around and fixed up for me and Katie. Mom was involved in anything that kept her close to her children.

She was a scoutmaster for the Cub Scouts and a chaperone for my sister's Blue Birds group. Speaking of my sister, Katie was the apple of mom's eye. She had been named after grandma, Katherine Marie. Katie, my sister that is, well maybe grandma too, was a right proper looking little Irish girl. Her strawberry blond hair ran down her back in thick waves. It was so thick that she was always pushing it out of her eyes, which were the color of emeralds. She was a picture, to be sure. I always thought that some guy, someday... but that day is never going to come.

─────

So now I have to dry my eyes again. Remembering my parents and my little sister always makes me tear up. So, I discard that memory and blink away the tears that are pooling. Mary's body is warm enough to melt most of the snow on the barrel, but the site, which is closer to me, has a little mountain on it. I could blow it off, but there is no reason to do so. I am kind of curious how much will accumulate before Mary barks and knocks it all off.

I casually grab another pinch of snow and pop it in my mouth.

─────

Where was I? Oh, that's right, we were in six days when we got our assignment. Essentially, we had four two-man teams going in to sit on a compound and wait for the bad guys to show up. Four teams were scattered in variant distances around the only vehicle gate in the compound. Once the cars got through the gates, we would have no shots. The walls were too high and the dirt that we were laying in was too low. There was next to nothing in this patch of sand, except for the compound.

We came up with a plan to get us in. It was not a great plan, but it was a plan. I cannot say that we executed the insertion plan with any kind of precision, however, we did manage to get all four teams inserted without alerting the locals. Once in, it was radio silence. It was silence, period.

Doug and I found a nice little group of scrub and burrowed in for the long haul. The cars were supposed to start arriving within the next twenty-four hours.

Until they arrived, we needed to be ghosts. We could not be seen, heard, or smelled. We could give nothing away. We all had Gilly suits that kept us hidden, but a very keen eye can catch improper movement or sounds that do not belong, and believe me, their security people are not as stupid or clueless as Hollywood makes out. We needed to be better.

Our body positions were in easy to hold positions as any movement that we make could be detected, we made as few movements as possible. When we did, they were minuscule. While one shifts an inch, the other remains completely motionless.

Our breathing was shallow and relaxed, with an occasional long pull of air. Followed by a full stop.

We would tense our muscles slowly and squeeze the blood out of them and then release them, this keeps them from cramping and being useless when we do need to move. If we are discovered, we will need to move, and we will need to move quickly. Stiff muscles are a death sentence.

We took tiny sips of water from our Camelbacks, so the fluid is more likely to evaporate from our skin, instead of lying in our bladders. Urinating causes an odor that is unmistakable. If we must urinate, we must do it in the position that we are in. Everyone has their own preferred method of accomplishing this task, and all those methods include almost no movement and laying or sitting in your own piss. Nobody likes this. It is just a fact of life. It is also probably the biggest reason that there are no women in the sniper units as yet. It is coming. Someone will come up with a bladder or something that allows snipers to pee without having to lay in it for hours or days. When that happens, they will probably start training female snipers in earnest. I hear that they train some now, but only in Guard or Reserve units. In other words, only in units that are not likely to deploy on missions like the one that Doug and I were on when we hunted the murderers in their lair.

Our breathing and movement became a type of irregular cadence for us. We no longer needed to concentrate on keeping this cadence, we are veterans at this game. Our attention was given to the task at hand, waiting for cars.

We waited for eighteen hours before the first car rolled up. The sun had begun to wane in the west, and we were both dripping in sweat. We could smell food cooking. It didn't smell too bad. Both our stomachs rumbled, and our mouths filled with water. We had eaten, but just energy snacks. They must have been making dinner for their guest.

Just before the first car came into view, we could see the trail of dust rising in the distance. The locals ran out of the buildings in the compound in force. We knew that there were a lot more of them than we had seen since arriving. Now they were all out to be seen by whoever was in the car. It was a good time to get a more accurate count of the bad guys, so we did. We assumed the other teams were assessing the new information as well. The voice in my ear, Doug, was only in my ear. Our radios were only for us. The other teams had the same. If we needed to talk to them, we would need to change things up.

The car angled up to the gate. It was not bullet proof. It was a remake of a 1940's gangster car, or maybe it was real. I really had no idea. I just don't like the idea that one of America's great iconic cars was in the hands of one of these Jack Asses. So, I called it a remake. It also made me feel better if I have to shoot the damn thing up, if it is just a remake.

Anyway, the car stopped at the gate and the driver popped his head out of the window like a Whack a Mole. He was talking to the guards. After some discussion and a few furtive glances towards the back seat, the gate swung open, and the car drove through.

We had not gotten a clear view of the passenger in the car, but it was a fair bet that this was not a very high value target judging solely upon the vehicle that he had been in. We were looking for the "bullet proof" car that warranted an escort.

And so, we waited. Just like I am waiting now. Barely moving or breathing. A human rock, waiting for the right car with the right target. I waited patiently for Doug to tell me adjustments based on the wind, heat, distance, and general topography. There are a lot of factors that go into a sniper's long-distance shot.

The car was inside with an escort of about a dozen of the guards as well as his own four-man entourage who had come in a banged-up Jeep trailing the Gangster car. The passenger was deposited in front of the largest building in the complex and the car drove around behind and disappeared. The man did not look around, so all I saw was the back of his head. He had a version of a high and tight, but the barber had carved a logo or something in the hair on the back of his head. Clearly, he was a younger man who was trying to make a fashion statement. As he disappeared inside, everyone else either followed or disappeared in other doorways and the compound became all but silent. It was reduced to low voices and muffled laughter mingled with the smell of roasted goat and Turkish tobacco as the sun disappeared and night fell. I adjusted my glass for darkness.

As night fell, the desert cooled quickly. One of the earmarks of high desert terrain, aside from the rocks, is the cold nights. The sun can cook you by day, and the moon will freeze your sweat. Laying on the ground, a pool of sweat forms under your body. Then the night comes and the sand that had so efficiently fried your skin just hours before now leached the heat from your body and turned your sweat into ice water. And Gilly suits do not help one damn bit with your personal comfort, of course they're not supposed to, but well...

It was not difficult to spot the headlights of the next car to crest the horizon. The compound was in the middle of nowhere. There was sand and more sand in every direction. The few patches of scrub brush, which we had found to hide in were only here because of the compound. Somewhere, probably under the place, either water was leaking or there was a moving body of water. That water had been found by the seeking roots of these plants.

The last passenger piled out with the rest of the rank and file as the first set of headlights arrived. His haircut was distinct. But this time I saw his face. If I remembered right, he was a security professional or he claimed to be.

This time, the gate was opened, the car drove through but did not go far. The passenger got out of the car and looked the gate guards up and down. He scrutinized the other soldiers and appeared to bark some orders that several of the men jumped to obey.

When he was satisfied with his brief inspection, he pulled out a phone and shortly thereafter more cars appeared on the horizon. The game was finally coming to a conclusion. My senses perked up a fraction more and my skin began to tingle. Anticipation, it was not about waiting for the Catsup to come out of the bottle. This was about the long wait being nearly over.

Soon we would all know who got to live and who did not. Pure mayhem would erupt the second after that first shot. That's when all bets must be in as there would be no turning back.

A cloud of dust rose for quite a distance behind the cars that I could see. I was angled almost dead on the front gate, where all of the cars that were coming from my right would need to at least move slowly. Doug had the optic. He was looking into each car as best he could at our angle.

The gate was the one true weakness of this compound. It was small, allowing only one car through at a time, and it was the only way for a vehicle to get in or out. There were a few man gates along the perimeter of the wall, but this seemed to be the only way for a vehicle to access the compound. The security personnel had opted for a more "Shelter in Place" kind of security system. I saw it as a fatal flaw that they chose a defense only style of security. They had guard towers and lots of firepower on the walls. But if they needed to get out quickly, they would be held to that one gate.

The cars were beginning to line up. The gate was just a fatal funnel. Some of the drivers coming down the road seemed to realize the error. They were stopping on the road and leaving a lot of distance between themselves and the car in front of them. It was becoming very clear that if we were going to take out a player, we would need to get it done very soon.

Four shots occurred almost simultaneously. We all had suppressors, so all anyone might have heard was the sound of air being spit. As far as I could tell, no one heard anything. Everyone did, however, see red mist blossom in a couple of cars as the rounds found flesh. My shot caused some red mist in the car that was sitting in the gate opening. I hit the driver. So, the car would be stuck in the gate.

I quickly chambered another round. Sadie, that was my name for my rifle, was a bolt action rifle with a 10-round clip. I fired again, taking out one of the gate guards. Then I shifted as I could hear rifle fire coming from the compound and could see sand dusting up about 25 yards in front of me. We were not out of their range, but hitting accurately with their rifles at this range, well that would be extraordinary. Still, there was a chance. I said, "Left corner tower." Doug readjusted and within a few seconds gave me some direction. I fired again. I did not make a kill, but I did give them something to think about.

We had completed our assigned task at least the other teams thought that they had, they were bugging out. Anyone else that we might have taken out would be gravy for the goose. But that would happen as we tried to extract ourselves to the LZ, where we were supposed to link up some local assets who would get us to an actual air lift. I know, LZ stands for Landing Zone, but there was no way in any scenario that we were landing anything that close to the compound. We were heading for locals with land vehicles. So, LZ was just the name that we gave it.

I say, supposed to, because it did not happen that cleanly. We were damn lucky it happened at all.

Doug and I were team number one, and closest to the LZ which was about two clicks away and the actual air lift was over five clicks further. It doesn't sound like much until you have been in this kind of situation. Anyway, it was the job of me and Doug to go last and cover the asses of the other three teams. But first, I took a couple more shots at the tower guns. I got a lucky shot on the fuel farm and got a small explosion for my efforts and then I peppered the gate with a few more shots. Then it was time to leave. I chambered my second clip before slinging Sadie over my shoulder and onto my back.

That sounded simple right? Let me tell you about my Sadie, all rifles can be sniper rifles. Some rifles were simply designed with only that application in mind. They were rifles, they can shoot anything in any way that the holder chooses. Sadie was simply not designed for rapid fire. She was a single shot bolt action M82A1 with a ten-round clip and she was a heavy girl. So, running with her, was a task. I had only brought twenty-one rounds with me. I did not expect to have the opportunity to use more, and I had been right. Sadie and I were done with only 11 rounds down range.

Anyway... we pulled out. I knew the other teams were scrambling towards the same rendezvous point. I could not see them. I did not need to. We had trained for hours upon hours together. We all knew how each other moved and thought. I knew where they would be before they got there, and they knew that Doug and I would cover their retreat.

From here on I used my handgun. I did not have time to stop, find a target and fire. Maybe later. We did not plan on hanging out for a long time. I counted in my head, not the rounds that I was expending, those would run out on their own without the need to count, no I was counting seconds. How long does it take to run a two click sprint while toting a 12-pound long rifle? I had counted while in training with this crew, I knew exactly how long, and hence I was counting.

———

Thinking back on this story is hard. It makes me angry, anxious, and sad all at the same time, only because I know how it ends.

12

Not a Good Plan

We had a plan, if we could get over the next dune, there was a natural water runoff area with exposed rocks and hard pack formations that we could use for cover while we made our way to the LZ. We could all hear the commotion behind us in the compound. It would take them a few minutes to clear the gate and that would be all the head start that we would get. The cars already outside the compound may or may not pursue, it depended on who was in them and if they would just want to bug out themselves. It did not seem like a long time, before we could hear the sounds of shouting men and vehicles gaining on us. They threw up flairs from their vehicles and when they saw something, their yelling got louder.

We ran, ducking, swerving, stumbling, and occasionally shooting over our shoulders in answer to the rounds flying around our heads. We seldom glanced back. What would have been the point? It only would have served to slow us down.

I could not see the others. Only Doug was still in my view. I could hear screaming. It was not behind me. One of our team had been hurt.

My legs began to burn. Running in sand is only fun if you are on a warm sunny beach. It is neither fun nor exciting when you are running for your life. When I crested the dune, it was like opening a Christmas present that you realized once you had excitedly ripped open, you did not really want what was inside.

On the other side of the dune was a Jeep, filled with six bad guys. I dropped to one knee, ejected the mag from my handgun and slapped in a fresh one. Without thought, I brought the gun up and began firing at the men in the Jeep. At the time, I did not notice that some of the other guys were also firing on the men in the Jeep from other directions. I also did not notice that Doug was not firing at all. Later, I would wonder how this Jeep full of men had gotten in front of us.

When all of the bad guys were down, I reached for Doug, who was about ten feet from me. He was groaning lowly. He had been shot in the leg. I could not tell how bad it was. We were in the shadow of the dune.

Pat yelled, 'Let's go!' Between us we threw our two wounded into the Jeep and while Pat was driving, the rest of us who were unhurt, pulled rounds and weapons from the dead bad guys and dumped the bodies over. Jake was the unit medic, it was not his job, he just filled the spot as he had been a field medic before he was a sniper. He tended to Bryce and Doug.

We were far from out of the woods. We were still being chased by somewhere between forty and fifty heavily armed men, and we were in their sandbox.

The Jeep was great in sand. But our plan was sending us into rocky terrain. It would not be a problem for the Jeep to navigate if we slowed down. We could not slow down by much.

The first decent rock caused us to go airborne. We landed with a loud crunch, and the sound of metal grinding over rock followed. Pat slowed down; I do not think that he had a lot of choice. Rocks seemed to crop up out of the sand like cabbage and the topography changed dramatically from a gently sloping dune to a wide crack in the earth. Either we had seen the wrong picture or there had been several flash floods in the last week to expose this terrain.

Bullets began to bounce off of the ground around us just as we heard the first echoing sound of gun fire, both rifle and handgun. Almost as one, we turned to see our attackers riding the rim of the overlooking dune. Where the rocks might have hidden men on foot from view, the Jeep definitely made us stand out. We could not change our hand now, without the Jeep, our wounded would slow us down and the delay would lessen their chances of survival, hell it would have lessened everyone's chances of survival. We all knew that the best that we could do under the circumstances was try to run. We had called in and given our situation and location. If anyone could help, they would be at or near the LZ. We had one click to go.

Doug told Pat to get us out of the valley, off of the rocks. So, Pat turned the wheel hard and headed us straight up the opposite side of the dune, away from our attackers. It was a steep climb and they rained lead on us the entire way. Many of those rounds found their targets.

From what I could see, Pat took one in the back plate. It knocked the wind out of him but that was all. I took two in the shoulder, they hit Kevlar and made my shoulder numb for a time, and then it hurt like hell. Jake took one in the back plate and one in the hip. Chase took one in the ear. We were all peppered with shrapnel from the Jeep and copper jacketing.

To his credit, Pat kept the Jeep headed in the right direction despite the blow to his back. He actually sped up and we caught some more air when we crested the dune. The Jeep bounced like a lopsided ball when it landed but, Pat got it aimed in the right direction and floored it. It jumped like a goosed ape and ran like a demon, dropping pieces of itself in the sand.

When we reached the LZ, we were met with a cadre of help. Men were quickly pulled from the Jeep and just when we thought that we could take a breath, out of the night we saw the red and orange tail of an RPG, heading straight for us. There was nothing that we could do but duck and cover.

When the smoke cleared, there was crap everywhere. The RPG had hit the Jeep. I found Doug under part of the rear axle and extracted him with some help. We got ourselves loaded onto the evacuation truck double time and were driving away when we saw the tails of two more RPG's. We did not wait around to see the resulting carnage.

Our allies called ahead. A chopper was waiting for us, and we were all Evac-ed to a nearby hospital.

—————

Days later, that is where I woke up, in the hospital. I had taken copious amounts of shrapnel to the left side of my body and my shoulder blade was fractured from the rounds I took, otherwise I was in good shape.

Al and Dustin came out with only minor shrapnel injuries. Dustin had bruised ribs from a round he had taken to the chest. Both men took extended leaves of absence then returned to their previous positions.

Jake and Bryce would live. Neither would ever be the same. The round that Jake had taken to the hip, shattered bone.

They remodeled it, but he would always need a cane. Bryce had taken two rounds, one in his thigh, it was a through and through, the second round hit him in the right wrist. Even with constructive surgery, Bryce would be using his left hand from then on. Both were given medical discharge.

Chase and Pat, Chase was gone. He had died on impact. Pat had only minor shrapnel injuries because Chase had been behind him and had gotten hit first. Pat had been covered in the blood and brain matter of his best friend, his brother-in-law, and the godfather of all three of his children. Pat stayed in the hospital long after his physical wounds had healed. He was given a medical discharge.

As for Doug, his leg wound was minor. Had it only been that wound... but it was not. The axle that landed on him had caused significant internal injuries. They did their best to patch him up. Some things just cannot be fixed. For Doug however, this was not the worst of it.

This is how it was told to me... When he came to, they handed him a phone. They had patched him through to Patti. She gave him something to live for, she was pregnant. It should have been the best news of the century for them both.

They wrapped him up and prepped him for the long ride home. He was in the air over the Atlantic when his heart stopped. The injuries had been too severe, and I slept through it all, again.

None of them had been expendable to me.

———

I breathe in and hold it. The snow continues. Tears of sadness and anger fill my eyes. I blink them away. My left eye will not dry. I came down with allergies a few years back and since then my left eye simply weeps most of the time, and at times like this, it just doesn't like to stop. It's a good thing that I am right-eye dominant.

After that debacle, I actually sought out Doctor Cane.

13

Our Fallen Brothers

Just as the others had gone home, so did I. It was the longest plane trip that I have ever taken. We had all opted to escort Chase Filipe McDermott home to his family and friends. We were not Color Guard, but in his will, he had asked for us, those who survived, to carry his casket and say some words over his grave.

Our other comrade, Douglas Kaelan Shelby was already at home. Patti had held up the funeral so that, we could carry him, and speak for him as well.

Like I said, it was the longest plane trip that I had ever taken. I had far too much time to think.

Both men had asked to be interred in their traditional family plots. Which meant upstate New York for Chase and the U.P. Michigan for Doug. They were held a week apart from each other. Chase was first.

The weather was turning in New York. The trees had begun to change colors. It was beautiful, and as such, it was a striking contrast to the darkness, clouds and cold that was in my heart. Chase was not my shooting partner, but he was my teammate. We were all very close. We all knew each other's families and everything about each other, well nearly. He was my brother, and I miss him every day.

We carried him into the church. He had been a Lutheran. It was a closed casket, of course. People came and touched the casket and cried and said words.

The next day, we took him to his grave. The "viewing" time was over. It was time to put my brother in the ground. This is where we all said something. I had written something down, but when it came time to read it, I could not see through my tears. I just said what was in my heart.

Before long, it was just me left with Chase's wife and his family. Jake, Bryce, and Pat were still in the hospital and everyone else had gone. His casket had been lowered into the hole. My tears had dried up, and I had been left with an ache in my heart that felt a lot like that hole in the ground looked.

I still had one brother to put into the ground. We all did. I stayed for the reception at Chase's mom's house. I had a hollow feeling, and I was not hungry or in the mood to console anyone or be consoled.

I sat outside on the patio for about an hour. I did not talk to anyone. I grunted and tried to smile when someone would try to engage me. Then, finally, I just knew that it was time to leave. I hugged Chase's mom and wife before I left. I know that I said something to them, I just don't remember what it was.

Michigan was much colder than New York had been. The cemetery there was much closer to Lake Superior than the cemetery in New York had been to the Atlantic. Some people claim that Lake Superior might as well be an ocean for how cold and unpredictable she is. I tend to agree. My family is from the hand of Michigan. Doug and I had found a common bond in that knowledge.

I do not know how this could have been any harder on me, but somehow, knowing the cities and towns that his family talked about, and breathing the familiar air of my home state, only made things harder. Then, there was Patti.

How could I face her? I had no idea, not then and sometimes, not even now. She made it even worse when upon seeing me, she threw herself into my arms and began to cry like a baby.

I have no idea how long we held each other. I had waited to see her. It was impossible to consider going to their home, so we met for the first time at the church. Doug had been Catholic. The tenants are so similar to the Lutheran ones; in this case they are nigh indistinguishable. It was almost like a deja vu situation. Except for Patti.

I had no words for her. I remember mumbling some kind of apology for letting Doug get killed. At the word "killed" she lost it again, and that was my fault too.

Her father pulled her off of me. Somehow, this both relieved me and made me angry. My emotions were a disaster area. So many things were going through my head, not the least of which was the fact that I had not been given a chance to say goodbye to Doug. He had just up and died when he was supposed to live. Who was going to be a father to his children? Who was going to hold Patti's hand during the hard months ahead? Should this responsibility fall to me? Would that be a betrayal of all that we had together as brothers? Would that be what Doug would want?

I was their son's godfather. His education and general care now fell to me, but did I dare presume to fill the same role for their unborn child, or for Patti?

All of this and more ran through my brain for days and weeks. Even today, I hear Doug's voice accusing me. Reviling me. Damning me. Blaming me. Hating me. Patti would make me an appointment for my shrink if she knew what I was thinking. So, I did not tell her. I would eventually tell Doctor Cane.

The "viewing" part was a blur. Other than the part in which I personally participated, i.e., the carrying in of my brother and the subsequent carrying him back out again, I remember nothing, not even the sound of a hymn.

By the grave site, I stood with Patti and their son. She held his hand and looped her other hand around my arm. When their son began to fuss, she picked him up and moved a few inches closer to me so that, our shoulders touched. I was her rock. I was a rock, inside and out.

Once again, we all said some words. This time I had no prewritten words to have in my hand. I also was dry of tears. My heart was so broken that my very soul felt ruptured and dead. I said only 10 words, "He was my brother, and I will miss him forever."

Everyone left, leaving only Patti and me standing beside a hole in the ground with a casket inside. I had not looked at my brother's face, even though it had been an open casket. His face was burned into my memory, along with his laughter, his voice, his words, his smell... I knew my brother, inside and out and he would be with me until the day I died. I did not need to see his inanimate face inside of a casket.

They never look the same. My parents and sister had looked like someone else. Now, when I try to remember their faces, all I see are their death masks. I did not want that for Doug. I had learned that lesson the first time around.

———

The little pile of snow on my front site seems to be growing. What are the odds of a snowflake randomly landing on the tiny front site of a rifle? I suppose that it depends upon the number of snowflakes in the equation.

Do you like the way that I distract myself? Dwelling on sadness or anger only deepens it. I do not have time for that right now.

14

Healing Takes Time

I did not feel normal. I knew that I was not acting normal, but damned if I knew how to tell my mandatory counselor what he wanted to know so he could fix me. If he could not fix me, then I could not resume my job. He would not clear me for duty, and the months dragged on. That is when I called Doctor Cane. She had not been my shrink, they don't call them that anymore, now they are counselors, but she had not been mine for several years. She had moved to Alabama to be near her ailing mother. But I called her anyway.

My visits to Patti were strained. She was understandably devastated. Her life was broken, and she was getting bigger, with Doug's child in her belly. She did not seem happy about it. How can that be good for an unborn child? I could see in Mikey that their house was not a happy one. I know that Patti's parents were doing their best to fill in the gaps. There were just too many gaps, and some were not the kind that parents can fill.

One day, about seven months in, I was visiting Patti. I had just put Mikey down for a nap when the General pulled me outside. We were alone. He said something that I will never forget, "Look son, you're broken, she's broken, we're all a bit broken. But you have the ability to fix us all, if you can pull your head out of your ass and do what you know is right."

I literally had no idea what he was talking about. How can I fix anyone if I am also broken? I think that I asked him as much. That's when he told me something that really rocked my world. He said, "We all know you are in love with my Patti. She knows it and Doug knew it. But no one ever said anything because you were such a gentleman about it. You never acted on it, not even with a look."

That was the most stunning news that I had ever heard. I thought I had played it so cool and here he was, the General, telling me that he knew and what was worse, Doug had known. And how could he not? He was my best friend. There was not a whole lot that we did not know about each other. I know that I stuttered out something that sounded just as lame in my head as it sounded out loud. Trying to deny the truth when you have been caught out is absolutely useless.

I tried to duck out of the conversation but, he was having none of it. He took me by the upper arm and said, "It's time for you to man up, son. My daughter needs a man, her children need a father, and you need them all."

What could I say to that? What could I do?

I looked again at how Patti had been acting around me. She knew! I was so embarrassed and angry with myself that I ran, like a coward. For nearly two weeks I did nothing but drink. I let my studies lapse, because of all the things that I had stopped doing, college was not one of them, but now that I was wallowing in self-pity, I let even that slide.

It was not until I received a phone call from the General telling me that Patti was in the hospital with one of those pregnancy complications that I finally did as he had told me to do, I pulled my head out of my ass, cleaned myself up and headed for the hospital.

I was never good at breaking the ice with Patti, but she had other plans. She took hold of the conversation the second that I walked into the room. It went something like this:

"Sit down Steven. Stop hovering and sit down."

I did as I was told. "How are you...?" I couldn't get much out.

"Feeling? I am glad that you didn't finish that question." She looked at me with those brilliant green eyes. She looked so very tired and there were a few streaks of grey in her beautiful hair. It had turned to a dark brown with her first pregnancy. Still, it was gorgeous, she was gorgeous, with that soft roundish face, the tiny dimple in her chin and her coffee and cream complexion, she was half Mexican and half Norwegian, and every bit of it showed on her face and in her personality. She had been watching me, watch her. She spoke softly, "Look Steven. I know that you are in as much pain as I am, maybe a bit more. But you have to know that you are not responsible for Doug's death."

"Patti, I... I couldn't stop it. I tried..." And that is when I started crying and my words stuck in my throat.

She reached out and took my hand. I scooched my chair closer, so much so that my tears fell on our hands. "I know that you tried, Steven. You loved him as much as I did, still do."

That is when my head met the bed and she put her hand on it while I cried. I have no idea how long we stayed like that, nor how long I cried. She just let me. When I could manage it, I lifted my head. She had been crying too. That was no surprise. "I'm sorry." I did not know what else to say.

"You have nothing to be sorry about. Doug loved you. He trusted you and I know that you did everything that you could to bring him back alive." A stab of shame pierced my heart.

"I was asleep when he died. I slept through it all... again." The weight of that shame wanted to crush me. First it was my parents and sister, then it was Doug. Who would be next?

She must have seen it in my eyes or something that I did. She leaned towards me and gripped my face in both her hands. "Listen to me, Steven Harrington. You were injured too. I don't know what I would have done had you both died. But you didn't. So... now we have what we have." She paused to put her hand on her belly. Clearly, she was in pain, physical pain, and here I was acting the baby.

I pulled away, suddenly very concerned for her. "What can I do?" I meant for the baby or whatever was ailing her. She did not take it that way.

"You can stop succumbing to survivor's guilt and help me." She put her hand on my face again. It was like electricity. "I know what you think of me." I must have flinched because her next words were commanding and caring at the same time. "Now stop! Don't be ashamed of how you feel. I am glad for it. In fact, had you worked up the huevos to talk to me at that damn party, I might have been given a chance to choose between you. But you never gave me that chance. Now, I am not giving you one. If you love me like everyone says, Steven Harrington, then hold me. Comfort me. Be the white knight that comes to my rescue, because God knows that I need rescuing right now."

I must have looked both stunned and horrified and I certainly could not speak.

"I know that you are terrible with words, unless you are quoting some regulation or something, so show me. Steven, I am scared, more scared than I have ever been in my life. If you love me and are willing to stand at my side and be a comfort to me and my children, then hold me. Be my rock." Somewhere in the middle of that burst of anger her voice turned to one of pleading. It was the most pleading voice that I had ever heard, and I had heard a fair few on the battlefield. For the first time since meeting Patti, I did not think, I just acted. I rose from my chair and sat on the bed next to her and I held her like I had always dreamed. It did not feel like it did in my dreams, it was real, she was real, and she was shivering from fear in my arms, so, I held her tighter.

After that, I simply took the part that Doug would have taken. I moved in with them, not into her room, but into the house, into their guest room and I did all the things that Doug had once done.

I potty trained little Mikey, mowed the lawn, fixed the fence, and painted it. I cleaned the pool, and I built their unborn child a nursery, just the way I thought that Doug would want it.

I held Patti's hand as she gave birth to their daughter and washed the baby's face when the nurse held her up to me. I smiled when Patti named her after her own mother and Doug's mother. She was and is Isabella Shannon Shelby. When the ladies came home, I treated them like the Queen and Princess that they were and when no one was looking, I cried with joy and shame, because of my joy.

The one thing that I never did, was touch anything that had belonged solely to Doug. It was not my place. I was just a cheap replacement for a hell of a man.

Somewhere in there, we all became accustomed to each other's presence, and we were all given a clean bill of health from our respective shrinks. We had become a semblance of normal, together, and apart. We were a kind of mismatched puzzle of a family, all leaning on one another for support.

That being said, I still spoke to Doctor Cane on the phone at least twice a week. I told my official counselor what he wanted to hear; I told Doctor Cane the truth.

When little Mikey told us one day that his name was 'Michael' not 'Mikey' and then called me "Daddy," our worlds scrambled. Patti fell silent and got an odd look on her face. Then, she went into the house and returned a minute later with her hand balled into a fist. She opened her hand and gave me the key to Doug's private "man cave." She had not entered it, that I know of, since before he was gone. We did not exchange words, but it was understood, what was once Doug's was now mine as well.

He had been gone about twenty months at that point. Michael's third birthday had come and gone, and little princess Bella had seen her first birthday.

After that little exchange, Patti started treating me like we were married. At first it was awkward, and I felt guilty, like I was cheating, or she was cheating. Then one day it came to me, if we started over, as if we were meeting for the first time, maybe our relationship would have a chance, maybe we could both move past the specter of Doug that hung between us.

A week after Michael had made his announcement, I asked Patti out on an official date. The General and Miss Esperanza were more than happy to watch the children while Patti and I went to an early dinner and a concert in the park.

The evening was magical. For several hours, we forgot all of the pain and trauma in our lives and became two infatuated people out on a date. When we went home, the weight of our lives crashed down upon us again, but somehow it seemed less weighty for us both. So, we made a weekly thing of it. We took turns deciding where to go or what to do. And after each date when we returned home the weight lessened. Until one day, it seemed gone altogether, and when that happened, I looked down at those beautiful green eyes and I kissed her for the very first time. No one stood between us anymore. Still, we were both shaking with anticipation and a bit of guilt and fear, but those last two disappeared when Patti led me by the hand into her room. We were hungry for companionship, closeness, comfort, and each other. That night, we feasted and laid our fears to rest once and for all.

I'm still holding my breath. Nothing has moved on the road. This is a much different assignment than the one that cost me the first two brothers that I lost. For one, I am not in a hot desert, clearly. Secondly, I am not forced to set up so close to my target. I am on a ridge, far from where my target is going to be. When my target turns to mist, I will be packing up. There will be no harrowing chase through rocky terrain, no bullets flying, no RPG's glowing in the night and none of my brothers will die. So, you hateful assholes can stick it, there are no expendables here!

Sorry, clearly, I still have some anger issues to work through.

That is not to say that we did not have any guilt. Patti worked on moving past the guilt that she felt over Doug's death. She blamed herself for him being distracted. It was tough convincing her that had it not been for her "distraction," Doug would never have been the man that he was. She was the best thing that ever happened to him, and that was the God's honest truth. Still, sometimes I would catch her just staring. Sometimes she would stare at Michael, who as he grew, looked more and more like his father and he had many of Doug's mannerisms. Sometimes, she would just stare at nothing, but she would have a wistful look on her face. This is not the way she looked at me. I had asked her many times, long before I asked her to marry me, if she had any regrets. I gave her the out. I told her that I would stick around and be whatever she needed, and she did not have to marry me. But, in the end, marriage is what she wanted.

When Michael was 10 years old, I adopted him and Isabella. They chose to hyphenate their names. They became Michael Shelby-Harrington and Isabella Shelby-Harrington. It was fitting, given their partial Mexican heritage. They asked me to become their "official" daddy on Father's Day. "That way we can get you really, for real Father's Day presents, because you really are our daddy. Doug was our Father, and we can't get him presents, not really, and you're our Daddy, Daddy and we like getting you presents." Thus was the logic of 8-year-old Bella. I did not understand the logic then, or even now. But I understood the love that was behind the request and I was truly honored to fulfill it.

Patti dove into their education. She became the ultimate soccer mom, with an SUV, a family dog and a bonified membership in the local PTA. She baked cookies and brownies and hosted after-practice Pizza Parties and even yelled at a few Teachers and at least one Principal that I know about. She went to all the games, meets or whatever they were calling the event. She even became the Manager of an extracurricular Softball Team for a few seasons and a Den Mother for the Cub Scouts. She never wanted the children to ever feel as if they had less because their Father had passed away. She had a little trouble with Bella's logic as well. The children never had any confusion about who I was in their lives or who Doug had been. It was Patti who for a long time had trouble with defining and accepting the new roles, even after I adopted them. Not that she would ever undermine my role in their lives, because for a lot of these things, I was with her, literally with her, at the game, picking them up after practice and taking them shopping for whatever they needed. This was more a balm for Patti than it was for the children, and we were all okay with that knowledge, well Bella was least okay than anyone else. For her, I was the only father that she had ever known and Michael had only a dim memory of Doug. It was more of a feeling or emotion really. But it was Bella who gave Patti her "come to Jesus" moment regarding my role in all of their lives. It was before I adopted the children by a few months and it was probably the reason that Patti bought into the idea.

The girls had gone to a Blue Birds get-together that included dinner, but it was a girls' only affair. Michael and I went to Pizza and the movies. When we got home the girls were already there and they were in the middle of a very loud argument.

We came in to this:

"No, mommy! Daddy is Daddy. You call him Daddy and you tell all of us that you love him. But then when people ask where my Daddy is, you tell them that he is in bed in the U.P. You know that's not true Mommy. My Daddy is right there!" She pointed right at me as Michael and I entered the room. "He's not... well I don't know what U.P. means or why you say that he is sleeping there, but it is not here! My Daddy is here!" And with that she ran over and attached herself to my leg and started crying.

I looked at Patti and said, "Do I dare ask?" She burst into tears and left the room. I looked down at Michael and said, "You go comfort Mommy. I got Bella." He nodded and followed

145

after his Mother. I reached down and picked up Bella. "I got you, baby."

Bella snuggled into my neck and cried for a while. When she was done, she leaned back to talk to me. "Daddy, why does Mommy tell people that you are in the U.P.? What is she talking about?"

"Hmm, well sweetie, you know that place we go to every once in a while, the place with all the big stones with words and names on them?"

She nodded. "The seminary."

"Yes, the cemetery."

"Ya, cemetery. That's what I said." She smiled evilly. I tickled her. "Oh wait, is that cemetery in the U.P. and do people sleep there? I don't remember seeing any beds."

"Yes, dear. It is in the U.P. and the man that we visit was your Mother's first Husband and your Father."

"Oh, yeah. I know all that." She said sagely. "But you're my Daddy." And that was the end of the argument. To her, Daddy and Father were two different things and her Mother needed to tell people that her Daddy lived with them and took care of them and did all of those things that are important to an 8-year-old girl. He most certainly did not sleep under a big stone with his name on it and that was that.

———

You know what? Maybe it was Michael's conversation with Patti that evening that started the conversation of adoption. I had never broached the subject. Maybe I should have, but I always figure that if Patti wanted me to adopt the children, then she would bring it up. Maybe she did, through Michael.

I love that I can think of my family and get a warm sense of peace inside my gut. It might never have happened had I not pulled my stubborn head from between my butt cheeks. I needed therapy. I had needed it since my parents and Katie had died. It took me a while to figure that out and even longer to find someone who I could confide in, outside of family and friends. Doctor Cane had been that person. You know what, I get a warm feeling inside my gut when I think of her too, most of the time, but sometimes I just want to laugh. Let me explain.

Ahh, Doctor C.S. Cane. I love that woman! She is really old now and the last time I saw her, just visiting, she finally told me what the C.S. stands for... wait for it... Candy Sugar Cane... I lost it and she hit me with a wooden spoon! Can you imagine? What exactly would possess parents to name their child in such a way? I am reminded of the Johnny Cash song from years ago, "A Boy Named Sue." This poor woman probably went through some serious teasing. No doubt that is why she uses her initials. Yet, I am still laughing and being hit with a wooden spoon every time that I see her, cuz she knows I am still laughing, even when I am not. "Okay, Candy hit me again!" My stomach actually tightens with the last unreleased giggle, yes, I said giggle. I need to think of something else or my mirth will shake the snow from the branches.

15

The Sessions with Doctor Cane

I made it sound organic and simple, as if time alone healed our hearts enough to go forward. I do not think time can heal wounds. Time gives us the space to work on healing.

I cannot even begin to express the anger and pain that I felt knowing that Doug had died while I slept. It was my parents and sister all over again. Survivor's guilt doesn't quite cover it, but for Doctor Cane it was a solid place to start.

Somehow, the Doctor was not surprised by my call. Maybe she remembered how we had clicked all those years ago. Maybe not. She never said. Anyway, I called her, and we had some small talk, then she asked me why I had really called her, and I told her. I talked to her like I had never done face-to-face. I guess it was easier talking to a telephone. I told her how the Op had gone all wrong and how Doug had died, but do you know what she keyed on? She keyed on the fact that I had slept through it again and had come out relatively unscathed. Like

I said, survivor's guilt doesn't quite cover it, but that is where she started.

You see, Psych Doctors don't have to be someone who has shared your pain or your experience. They need to be someone who you can speak to, someone who listens and that ultimately, someone you will listen to. They do what the Army does, they tear you down to your base parts, and then they rebuild you. But they do it with your emotions. How you feel about something is gold to them.

I told Doctor Cane how I felt about sleeping through the death of my best friend. Was I feeling guilty, yeah you could say that, but not because Doug had died, and I had not, but because I felt relief when I thought of Patti. Finally, the competition was over. Patti could be mine if I had the balls to take her. And that, ladies and gentleman, is the wrong thing to think.

This is why every time I looked at her, I broke down. I wanted to hold her and comfort her and I wanted her to do the same with me. But I wanted to keep her. My best friend was not even cold yet and I was coveting his wife. Let's be honest. I had always coveted his wife.

Doctor Cane actually sounded like she understood. She said that it was not uncommon and that my feelings were normal. I had been jealous of Doug. We both knew it and we both said it. He had the life that I had wanted. He had a Wife and a child and a home, and that was the real crux of my issues, Doug had a home. I had an apartment. I didn't even have a pet. And that was another issue that Doctor Cane hit on, why do I not have a pet? Not even a fish or a lizard? Was I that afraid of the pet dying when I wasn't looking? Yes, yes, I was that afraid of losing any semblance of home, so I did not make anything that looked like a home. I had an apartment with only a few pictures and sparse furnishings. I never invited anyone over. I did not even have a television. It was 720 feet of mostly unused space in a less than desirable area of town.

Doug had a home and Patti was the image of that home. Maybe, I only wanted Patti, because if I had her, I would have a home again. That's what the Doctor said. I argued a little with her. I had seen Patti first, I had just been afraid to talk to her. That's when the Doctor asked me, why was I so afraid of a girl? I had talked to other girls and even had relations with them. Why was Patti different? She was different because she was the girl who I wanted to keep. She was the girl who I would make a home with. And she was the girl who if I did all of that, I would be afraid to lose. That is why I was jealous of Doug. He had not been afraid to make a home.

Home. Everything kept coming back to that word, that concept, that which I had lost when I was fifteen. Places were not home, people were home. I had that much right. I was afraid to lose them when I was sleeping. That was part of why I could not sleep. The other part was the horror of what I had seen and done while in the field.

Doctor Cane said that I had quite the dilemma to unravel. I did bad things, or things that were contrary to my conscience while in the field and most people would have some relief going home. But I had not made a home to go to, so I had no relief from all of my wrongdoing. I had trapped myself on an endless treadmill. And the real kicker for me was when the Doctor told me that my love or obsession with Patti, was my mind adding a level of torture to my soul.

I was deliberately fixating on something that I was actively denying myself, a home. I would not be comforted. I was refusing that safety net to myself. When Patti was trying to help me find a girl, I had already decided that I would not accept any kind of comfort. Those attempts would always fail. I had preordained it to torture myself.

So, Doctor Cane asked, what event had occurred in my life that made me want to torture myself? That was a good question. Did it all really come back to survivor's guilt? When my parents and sister died, did I still carry that weight, guilty for their deaths because I was alive?

Doctor Cane was kind. She took my calls whenever I made them. I paid her of course. I did not tell the military that I had chosen a different doctor than the one that they had assigned me. All they knew was that that doctor was doing miraculous things with me. He was also working with Patti. But like me, Patti did not open up to this man.

While I was acting out and getting drunk, Patti was closed off and shutting down. That was not good for her unborn child. As I said, that was about the time that the General dropped that bomb on me. I went on that big bender, what I didn't say was that I made several drunken calls to Doctor Cane. We had already gotten to the self-torture stuff, so when I told her that Doug, Patti, and her parents all knew that I was in love with her, she actually laughed.

"What the Hell!!!! How can you be laughing at me?" I yelled into the phone.

She sputtered a bit and said, "You have been laboring under a false umbrella of anonymity. You are more transparent than you know. How could they not see? Steven, it is time for you to stop being selfish and reach out to Patti. You don't have to marry her, just be there for her. The General is right. She needs your strength and support and if you are too afraid to give them to her, then you need to leave and never see her again."

I did not know how to respond to her. I thought for a long time over those words. Finally, I said, "I think that I need her too."

"I think that you are right. So, what are you waiting for? Put the bottle down. Sober up and go help someone other than yourself."

That is what I did. Well, I started to, but then I got that phone call telling me that Patti was in the hospital. So, technically, I had made the decision to sober up and help her out before I knew that she was in the hospital. It all happened about the same time.

Well, you know what happened at the hospital, I went in with every intention of doing what Doctor Cane had told me to do, stop being selfish. It did not matter that I was embarrassed, afraid, or guilty, all that mattered was Patti. But, well, Patti took the wheel.

I was really bad about talking to Patti, but to be honest, it was Doctor Cane who helped us both out. We both had issues. Patti felt very guilty about needing me to fill in the gaps and to hold her. I had issues with creating a safe place for myself. But we both worked on it, sometimes together and sometimes apart. I actually felt bad for Doctor Cane, she fielded more calls from the two of us than she should have. But she stuck with us through all of the hard decisions for the next two years.

When Bella was born, I felt like I could never be happier than at that moment. But there were a hundred other moments after that day that somehow trumped it. Doctor Cane and Patti helped me work through the guilt of being happy with another man's family. Still, it took a lot of work for me not to feel like a usurper or an inadequate substitute.

At the same time, Patti felt like she was betraying Doug by needing my help. The truth was that she had always harbored a few feelings for me as well. She had often wondered who she would have chosen, had I worked up the huevos and spoken to her. But that was between us, I hope. Anyway, her parents did what they could to assuage her feelings, but it really was the one-on-one sessions with Doctor Cane that let Patti work through her feelings. I guess it was easier for the both of us to talk to a phone.

In the end, Doctor Cane helped us both to understand that gain and loss are what life is all about. We gain a car and trade it in a few years later. People are not cars, but they do not stay in one place. People move on, either in life or in death and we who remain must accept that we are not to blame for their absence in our lives. We honor their contributions to our lives by us living to our fullest. Our pain, guilt, sorrow, or need cannot bring the dead back. We can only move forward and build upon those parts that they left behind that we can use.

Patti and I built a life for the children that Doug left behind. We did not lose ourselves in the children, but we did not exclude them either. Patti and I and the children became a family, a disjointed and slightly lopsided family, but a family that loved each other, not despite or because of anything. We simply accepted each other for who we were and as we were.

These were the findings of Doctor Cane regarding my attachment issues. We touched on my other issues, but the real focus for these sessions was all about survivor's guilt and how that can balloon into a self-destructive monster that eats happiness for lunch. Does that mean that I don't miss my parents and sister? Be serious. I will always have a hole in my soul where they once lived. But now I no longer let the hole become an abyss.

Does this mean that I no longer feel a bit of guilt when I lay down next to Patti at night? Again, be serious. Doug had the courage when I had not. But we have no ghosts in our house.

That ghost was finally laid to rest when Patti and I dated each other without inviting Doug's specter to tag along. We all knew what everyone's role was in the house and Doug graduated from a haunting ghost to a fond memory who we visited several times a year. This is how we all came to terms with Doug, his death and what kind of impact we wanted him to have in our lives. It was what Doug would have wanted, that we find each other in some manner and let him go, and so we have.

⸺

A breeze has picked up. Snow is swirling around us and making my glass a bit of a mess. With the smallest of movements, I clean it off. I think about that truck with the chickens. If that was a forward scout, then they really did not see us, or they set up and are still watching. This spot that I chose, is the perfect place for a sniper, and hence the perfect place to watch. Still, nothing is moving.

⸺

Time sometimes works backward. As the children grew, they began to understand the difference between Father and Daddy, if there was one. We never wanted to keep the truth from the children like some parents do. They needed to know, even before they truly understood. It is a hard pill to swallow, especially for children. But if you help them to understand when they are young, they most likely will not have the trauma to deal with as adults. I have seen families that waited to tell their children that Daddy or Mommy really wasn't their Daddy or Mommy. We never wanted that trauma for our children, at the same time, we did not want the children pining over a man that they never knew. It was a balancing act, and to be honest, it was precarious at times. We never forced anything down their throats, well there was the whole Brussel sprout thing, but that wasn't as big a deal as it was made out to be. Mommy and Daddy were just frustrated with the two-year-old with the fussy palate and big brother should have stayed out of it.

16

Moving Forward, Together

We all learn by doing. Some learn better than others, or faster than others. The military learned from the mistakes that had gotten our unit into so much trouble, and two of us killed. It took them a while, still they considered the price that they paid had been worth it. That was and is a point that we still disagree upon.

As a family we learned also, we learned that we needed to get away from the constant, in-your-face reminder of Doug. He was in our hearts and our memories, and that was enough. I needed to be my own man, my own kind of Husband and Father, not a wonky replica of Doug. That particular strategy, filling-Doug's shoes, had worked at first, when the wound was fresh and still bleeding, but it just could not work for the long haul.

Patti and I both needed a new start, and even though the children were young, we felt that they needed one as well. As I said, we do not keep that truth from our children, we never have. We wanted them to be comfortable with the facts of their heritage and to have access to their father's grave, so we moved. This was after the adoption. We moved to Sparta, Wisconsin, and I transferred to Fort McCoy. Michigan was right next door.

Now that they are older, they visit their father's grave whenever they want instead of making it a family thing, they can make it personal.

The house that we found in Sparta, had space, inside and out and we really needed that space to breathe.

We were about a mile from a really nice lake, not one of the Great Lakes, but a nice little inland pond. We were not so close that we needed to be concerned about the kids just falling in one day, but close enough that I could go fishing if I wanted. I had never wanted before, but who knew what I might want to do?

It was a two-story farmhouse that came with a little over two acres of green. The sight of it on that small hill surrounded by trees, shrubs, flowers, and grass made my heart pause. It must have struck a chord with Patti as well. When we stepped out of our rental to meet with the real estate agent there was a soft, warm smile on her face. But I think that it was the inside of the house that really sold her. The inside had been completely remodeled to accommodate all of the latest of everything. On the outside it was mid-century charm, while on the inside it was a modern haven. Patti told me, not asked me, to make an offer on the property immediately. I did, and since I had been banking paychecks for years, it was fairly easy to outbid the competition.

It was easy settling in. I was familiar with Wisconsin, having grown up next door and Patti was a chameleon when it came to fitting in. The house was not far from Fort McCoy, the base where I worked. We had decided against base housing, for personal reasons. Patti may be a chameleon, but living so close to so many other military personnel, would have caused a strain on both of us. Yet, this was something that the new shrink had problems with.

"Don't you think that you could use the extra support right now?" the new shrink asked, the new shrink we got when we moved.

"No, I do not think that we need a gaggle of geese up in our business. It's bad enough that we got you!"

Of course, I got the stink eye from the shrink and a knowing smirk from Patti for that one.

Shrinks have their place. Unfortunately, sometimes, they think that their place is up your ass and in your face. I personally do not think that every little feeling needs to be spread out like frosting on their cupcakes. Now, to be honest, sometimes talking about stuff helps you work through it. I am just not a fan of laying out my life to some random stranger. I do not care how many fancy pieces of paper she has on her wall or how comfortable her couch is, she is still a nosey busybody.

She asked me if I felt remorse or guilt after killing someone. I told her that I do not feel either. It is a job. The person on the other end of my round is a murderer, and my round is justice. Do I lose sleep over it? No, I do not. I lose sleep over the memory of pulling Doug out from under that rear axle, or the memory of seeing Chase's head explode. I see the blank stares of my brothers, the torn flesh, and the missing limbs. I hear their cries of pain and their pleading voices asking for help. This is what haunts my dreams, not pulling the trigger on a murderer. I worked through all of that crap with Doctor Cane years ago. But as that was off the books, this shrink didn't know, and I wasn't telling.

Chance and Doug were not the last of my brothers that I put into the ground, but I did not react the same with the rest. It is one thing to become callous to fake death, movie death, or video game death, it is quite another to become callous to real death. But that is the person that I allow others to see. I had learned that a person only has so much grief and when confronted with using so much of it, you learn, at least I learned that when that grief was spent, I could put on a mask that made others believe that I was stoic and strong. I was not. I had just come to the end of my grief and chose not to allow my face to keep wearing an emotion that was spent.

Did I feel it when we put, Jamie, Jon, Todd, and Kevin in the ground? Of course I did, and yes, I have lost sleep over it. But no one sees it. Well, Patti sees it, but to others, I am a blank. There were no tears to be had or given, not by me. I was a rock, just like I am when I am getting ready to squeeze the trigger. My shrink says that is not a good thing. She tells me that I have to "work through my feelings" so that I can be whole. I do work through them, just not with her. After all of the hours with Doctor Cane after Doug died, Patti and I learned how to help each other work through things. We became each other's rock and sounding board.

Honestly, I am not entirely certain who the shrink is trying to make me become. I am who I am, is that not good enough? I love my wife, I love my children, I kill without malice in my heart, most of the time, and I go to church every Sunday and on holidays, when I am not on mission. Still, my shrink thinks that I need to work on some issues, so, I let the shrink talk and I tell Patti all that I am feeling, within reason. I know that I have said that soldiers do not tell their wives about what they do unless they want a divorce. But Patti is the daughter of a military man and she was married to a man who was killed in

160

action and then she married the man that put her first husband in the ground. I think that she has shouldered enough to understand and not freak out. She agrees with me and has asked for me to confide in her.

Moving bases, of course, caused me to change units. It was a good idea. It helped me to heal and move forward with my life, and with our lives together. I finished college and got a bachelor's in business. Then, I did the paperwork and put on butter bars—that's a first lieutenant for you civilians. I was finally an officer.

As an officer and a decorated sniper, I had some choice in who I worked with. Oh yeah, as a survivor of that debacle I got a medal, a couple actually. I keep them in the drawer and dig them out when I have to wear my dress uniform. Al and Dusty had taken my cue and gotten their own butter bars, and both had changed their MOS, that is their job descriptions. Now they ride desks. Pat never came back to the military. He did go to school and got involved in a business that made medical aids for combat veterans. I saw them all occasionally and spoke to them more frequently on the phone. They all got their medals too. I think they keep them in their sock drawers. It really is hard to look at them for us all.

My new base already had a sniper unit, and they had a commanding officer. There was no room in the small unit for another officer. So, the Army saw fit to put me in the MP unit, under a man who had just made major. Now, this did not mean that I did not still train with the snipers, but I did so as an MP, not a Lieutenant. I was respected for my rank, but I was not in charge of anyone, not even myself. This group was newly formed, so they were different than what I was accustomed to. When they trained, they mixed up the teams a lot. Also, the Officer in charge, did not shoot or spot. He just organized the teams. So, he was mixing it up, seeing who worked best with who. My new partner became Dan Chin. Now Dan was a combat vet who had seen some gnarly stuff and was essentially just finishing out his 20 with this gig. We will get back to Dan later. He most certainly deserves to have a few words said about him, but right now we are talking about moving forward as a family.

I do not know if all of this will ever make full sense to me. I know that I am better now than I have been since that accident when I was a teenager and I only know that after this mission, if I can stretch it out to stay in country for another twelve days, I can glide into sanctuary before my rotation comes back around. Once in sanctuary, I can begin my out-processing. Then, I can put my business degree to use on a new restaurant that serves beer and wine with a nice dinner.

I cannot help but smile at the thought of retirement. They promoted me just before I left home about ten months ago. I put on light Colonel. And no, no kind of Colonel is supposed to be doing what I am doing right now, but I asked for this and after a few arguments, they let me have it. I do know that I will never make full bird, but I will stay in long enough to retire with the light Colonel pension. That is a big plus. I stayed in an extra five years to get this retirement. I will be forty-two. That restaurant sure is looking nice.

In my earpiece, I can hear Mark breathing. He is my new partner. He has been around for the last couple years. Mark is young, smart, and driven. He is also a pretty good shot, and he has eyes like an eagle, which makes him a great spotter. I have never let him be the actual shooter, not when I was with him. Of course, he has been the shooter a lot of times, but not when I am his partner. I do not wish that on anyone. My nosey shrink would love to hear that statement. When I talk about my "nosey shrink" I am not talking about C.S. Cane.

I glance in his direction. It is just light enough to see his silhouette against that anemic tree. He has his binos trained on the road. I blink and my eyes are back on my glass. I didn't need a spotter on this run. It is deliberately a milk run. I brought him because the Army told me to. When I retire, Mark will get a new partner and carry on. At least he is not putting me in the ground, he's putting me out to pasture. He does not know it yet, but that is the best gift in the world.

One thing that we learned from the new shrink, was that we could achieve a sense of normalcy if we developed a routine as quickly as possible. The routine would need to be uniquely ours, without any semblance of "what she did, or I did with Doug." Some things could not be avoided, like eating or sleeping, things like that, but we could make those times different as well. We could develop our own favorite meals, buy different dishes and flatware, and buy a new bedroom suite. We shopped for new furnishings and accessories together, that way it was "ours." We tried to do everything together, just the four of us. In that way, we became our own family.

Essentially, when we moved, we dumped almost all of our previous lives, in favor of a new one together.

At first, it was difficult. On the bright side, the move definitely made some of the redecorating easier. It was the smaller things. The personal things that we found hard to deal with.

It is easy to give a kitchen full of wedding gifts to charity, it is not so easy to put the jewelry box that Doug gave you in a box and put it in the attic. Neither of us could give that away. We decided that Patti could give it to Bella when the time was right.

There were quite a few items that were relegated to the "we'll deal with it later" category. Most were gifts, but we also put wedding picture albums and some of Doug's personal effects in that category.

We settled into a routine. It was a good routine. I got a full-time slot on base. It meant more pay and a permanent job, not a rotational job, but I could still deploy. It also meant that I could finish my schooling and as you know, I did finish and put on Officer.

The snow is thinning. For about half-an-hour there, I could not see anything, let alone a car a mile down the road. Good thing this guy is taking his time, I guess.

17

One More Down Range

Michael and Bella call me Dad. It is a good feeling. There is that word again, "feeling." It does not matter to me that they are not my blood. They are mine, and they are his, and I am okay with all of it.

Patti asked me once if I wanted one of my own. She even volunteered to allow a surrogate to carry our child if I would not want her to do so. I told her, "No." I was content, and I was not lying. I do not think she understood it at the time.

Most men have a natural drive to reproduce, to have a son to carry on their name. I do not care. I cannot explain it, but I feel completely content raising my brother's children at Patti's side. I could do this for the rest of my life and never feel that I have missed anything. This is the one thing that my shrink tells me is somewhat healthy, somewhat. That means that she does not really get it.

Patti gets it now. She feels the same. We are happy together, and in that happiness, we honor Doug's memory, and we raise their children to be good, and honest, and loving people.

One last mission. One more round down range at a real target. After this, I can shoot at paper and metal for the rest of my days. One more that is all.

It is amazing how much more time you spend reflecting on your life as you approach retirement.

Personally, I think we do this because we are approaching a time when our life is changing dramatically and, in some ways, we are allowing that part of our life to die, and we are moving on to do something else. At least that is what I hope is going to happen. I will be more than happy to put much of my present life to rest. Perhaps then, I will also find some rest.

———

Mark has not moved. His breathing is slow and steadily irregular, just like mine. He is a good partner. I will miss him when I retire. Part of me will miss this. When I am on mission, I feel like I am helping the world. I am making it safer, better. At home, I try to get that same satisfaction from raising Michael and Bella to be amazing and kind. I try to teach them the right values, the values that Patti and I share along with the General and Miss Esperanza and well hell, their entire family.

———

Let me take some time to tell you about the General and Miss Esperanza. Miss Esperanza, I call her that because she is so much more than just Mrs. Erickson or the General's wife. She is a force to be reckoned with. She is kind and strong and she has never met a child that she doesn't love on sight. Miss

166

Esperanza is the very embodiment of generosity, love and understanding. When I was running around with my head up my ass and the General had to tell me to remove it, it was Miss Esperanza who sometimes literally and most certainly figuratively held my hand. It was she who cleaned up my puke, washed my clothes and sometimes my ass. She fed me and cared for me as if I were one of her own children and she never once blinked when I reviled her or yelled obscenities at her. I even spit in her face once, an act that I will eternally regret and have repeatedly apologized for. She just wiped it off and offered me a glass of water.

Throughout the years, Miss Esperanza was both a rock and an anchor that helped to keep both Patti and me steady. You would think that the General would be those things, and he has been, but in a different way. I guess you can say what my shrink says, Miss Esperanza came to represent the mother I had lost and still needed. I have no idea. I have nothing to compare it with. I will say that she does embody the memories that I have of my mother. I can only surmise that if she had lived my mom would have been like Miss Esperanza. Mom was the voice in our family. Dad was quiet. It was Mom who cleaned our cuts, wiped our eyes, and made us cookies. It was also Mom who doled out punishment when it was appropriate and set the rules. She was the home keeper, the child raiser, and the Sheriff. Dad was the judge who only got involved when Mom brought it to him. Sometimes Dad intervened when he thought that Mom's judgment was too severe or if he had seen something that she had not. Sugar and spice, but not in the usual assumed arrangement, that was my Mom and Dad.

I am not certain that my Dad would have ever been like the General. The General became our compass, just as he was for all of his children. He set the course for us all and gave us the means with which to stay the course. It was Miss Esperanza who helped us up when we stumbled and ran interference with the General when we wanted to stray a bit off the path. My dad was a quiet guiding hand. He let us find our own path without a whole lot of guidance. He taught us right from wrong and how to be patient and loving. That was his guidance. It did not matter what path we chose in life, so long as we did it with all our hearts and exercised patience while doing what was right, we were good to go. I think that was a good thing. It was definitely a different approach than the General, but if push had come to shove, my dad would have stepped in. He always did when I was younger, I imagine that it would not have changed as I grew.

I suppose that I can see what my shrink has told me concerning the General and Miss Esperanza. They effectively came to be the parents that I had lost. I had never realized how much I missed my parents and their influence in my life until these two amazing people entered my life and even before Doug passed, they had stepped into that empty place and filled it with their love and concern.

Do not misunderstand. When people are yanked out of your life, they leave a hole. It is a deep dark emptiness that cannot be filled by anyone else. But other people can stand next to that hole and shine their light into its depths so that it does not hurt as much anymore. Sometimes their light is so great that they can seem to fill that hole, but they do not really, they make their own place and shine so brightly that the holes left by others can heal over. Do not tell my shrink that I just said that or she will think that she's getting through to me. Maybe she is, but I am not telling her.

———

I know that when I get home, Miss Esperanza will be there ready to greet me at the airport along with the General, Patti and our children. Miss Esperanza and the General will go home early that first night and not come by again for four or five days and then we will have a big meal together. I might be home for Christmas, which would be wonderful. I will be cutting it close with the way our flights often get delayed or messed up. They will want to send me to Germany or England or something, but I have already requested to pause the debrief until after the holidays. I still have not received an answer to that request. I guess I will see.

———

The road is still empty, except for snow. This guy sure is taking his own sweet ass time!

18

Giving Patti Time

Between the dating and me adopting the children, Patti and I needed some space from each other. She was having trouble working through something that I clearly could not help her with. She even flew down to Alabama to personally see Dr. Cane. When she came home, she had a stack of homework that she was very keen on completing, and she did not need me for that, at least that is what she told me. So, I put in for a "safe" deployment that got me sent to Norway. My mission was to teach some of their troops how to jump out of a plane. I was a good jumper back then; I guess that I still am. Just that now, I do not jump as often as I once did. It hurts more now than it did then.

Anyway, it was a pretty straightforward assignment. Spend three months in Norway doing jump training. It was a good gig. We folded a lot of silk and drank a lot of mead. They were big boys, made me look like a toy. It was fun calculating the weight ratios and even more fun jumping out some of their planes into terrain that looked a lot like where I am at now.

We hit more than one tree, but I will be damned if those guys were made of Iron Wood or something because, the worst that they got was a few sprained wrists and big ass bruises. I think that they actually hurt the trees more than the other way around.

The Russians heard about our escapades, the jumping ones, and I was asked by the local garrison, the one right across the ice from Norway, to come and train their guys how to jump as well. It was an official request, so I forwarded it to my upper-ups. The request was granted, so, when I was done drinking mead and hitting trees, I went over and trained some Russians.

Now that was an experience. The Russians had this old plane, and when I say old, I mean OLD. This thing had been built during the last World War and had not been kept on mothballs. No, this poor plane had seen better days thirty years ago. I honestly believe that I felt safer after I had jumped than before.

On the first day, I was surprised that it made it off the ground. It rattled, and creaked, and shook, and shifted, and bounced down the runway. I was expecting it to shake itself apart and leave us in a heap of metal and flesh at the end of the runway, but it caught air and lifted.

The noise and discomfort did not stop just because we were in the air. If anything, it became more terrifying. The damn Russians must have seen the disbelief on my face because they laughed so hard that one of them had a coughing fit.

This plane was like one of our Air Force C-130's. It had a back ramp, not a door from which to jump. They have doors, but the ramp is more efficient and safer. On this plane however, all of my previous apprehensions were decimated when the ramp dropped on this thing. The plane shook like a dog shakes a chicken by the neck. I was having a hard time continuing to keep my already jeopardized "cool." Certainly, this thing would shake the ramp door off. But no, it did not happen and before I knew it, the light turned green, and we began our jump. I could not wait to jump out of that plane! As instructor, I went last. It was a long wait, to be last.

I regained my composure in the air. This was my territory. One of the Ruskies puked. It was nasty, especially when one of his comrades flew through it. That part was actually pretty funny. I took a picture. It does not do the event justice. Other than the puke, that first jump was fairly successful. We got one turned ankle and that was it. We all celebrated with vodka, which is so much better in Russia and a damn site stronger than the strongest mead.

We jumped out of that rickety old plane a few dozen more times, but I always had a double shot of the strongest vodka before I got into the damn thing. And no, I never puked.

I stayed in Russia for nine weeks. Their training was a bit more intense, and we jumped a lot more. By the end, I was pretty accustomed to their old training plane. It was a hunk of junk, but it was a reliable hunk of junk, and it was a good excuse to drink.

After Russia, I was transferred to our Embassy in Italy. There was some Italian military that needed to learn how to fire a sniper rifle, and I was just the person to instruct them. I was officially deployed out of the American embassy in Italy.

We spent three weeks on the range, learning our weapon systems and each other. Then, I took them out into the field for two weeks. It was hot, muggy and the natives had more trouble with it than I did. They learned how to care for their weapons before they tended to themselves. In the field, a good solid, dependable weapon can save your life. Some of them learned that lesson quicker than others.

Back at home base, they got to clean their weapon systems for three days straight. Each day they came away with more grime than the time before. Finally, when one two-man team was able to put a Q-Tip into the feed ramp and come away clean, I let them all have a day off. To their credit, they all cleaned their weapon systems again on their day off, and they helped each other. It was the first real sign that I got that they were becoming a team.

Training snipers takes time. It is nothing to teach someone how to shoot a rifle. It is an entirely different thing to teach a group of people to be a team, and an even greater thing to train them how to be a sniper team.

I spent many months in Italy. I learned a little Italian and trained a pretty decent sniper team. I also got a bit homesick so, when Patti asked me to come home, I did.

When I made stateside, I had been gone for fourteen months.

The snow has muffled all sound. I can almost hear the trees breathe.

Those fourteen months were short and long at the same time. I feel that the time I spent at home with Patti and the children was good for all of us as a family, a new cock-eyed family, but deploying without a team, that time I spent just training people and letting loose that helped me to decompress. I had no life-or-death decisions to make. I had no live targets to eliminate. All I had was me teaching a bunch of guys from different countries how to do different things. And when it was time to go back to Patti, I did.

19

Triggers

As I have said, I was a decorated combat veteran and Officer, and my father-in-law was a two-star General. That means that I pretty much could get any deployment that I wanted, kind of like the one that I am on right now in Afghanistan. So, for years, after Doug was lost and I pinned on Officer, I took short, quick deployments. There was a time when I wanted action, adventure, and overall mayhem. But then I grew up, became a Husband and Father, and became a responsible man, or as the General often says, "Pulled his self-effacing head out of his ass." I had a reason outside of my own desire to continue to breathe, to come home. I had a home. So, I stopped taking unnecessary chances.

That is not to say that trouble did not occasionally find me on a deployment. There was that one time in Al-Falluja when my spotter and I got caught up in an ill-fated coup. Some idiot local thug, who thought that he had the huevos to take over the city with his gang started a gunfight in a very busy part of the city.

We were working at the US Embassy at the time doing somewhat sneaky grunt work for the ambassadorial staff. When while we were out in the city delivering an attaché to a different local thug, bullets started flying in all sorts of directions.

The first thug and his gang started firing at some local military. The second thug along with his cousin and their crew started firing at the first thug's guys. The Army guys could not tell one gang from the other, so they started firing at both. Well, that move got the second thug to also fire at the Army guys. This unusual cross-kinda-fire thing caused some other thugs, who may or may not have been affiliated with someone, to start firing at everyone they could see, including civilians who had no idea what the hell was actually going on. Me and Dan were included in this odd civilian group who just wanted to get out alive. It's still not time to talk about Dan.

We, along with several others, were scampering from one cubby hole to another trying to leapfrog ourselves out of harm's way. Many of this group were getting clipped or down-right filled with lead while attempting to scurry out. Why did we not just go inside you ask? Well, because when the bullets started, all of the shopkeepers locked and bolted their doors, and they were not opening up for anyone. So, there we were, armed, but forbidden from engaging, being shot at because let's face it, we were too light to be natives and were therefore targets, and making ourselves as small as possible while still moving away from the hail of lead.

After several harrowing minutes that felt like hours, we found ourselves scampering up a set of outside stairs. Once on the roof, we could make a mad dash across the rooftops to safety. It took a nurse nearly an hour to pick the rock and mortar out of my arm and back. At least it wasn't a bullet. I am thankful.

If you had not noticed by now, I am the kind of person who handles his issues by avoiding them. But some things cannot be avoided, mostly because they get thrown in your face when you least expect it. These things are called triggers, and most combat vets have them. Triggers are things that cause an anxiety reaction in us, and they can be anything, from a sound, a smell, or large crowds. When we get triggered, we react. Our reaction is based upon the trigger. If, for example, we hear sounds that mimic gunfire, we are most likely going to pull a gun and find cover and concealment and start looking for the bad guy. That is extreme. But it is real.

Most of us come home with a couple of things that cause us anxiety. The most prevalent ones are the ones that are triggered by seemingly innocuous events. For example, when we enter a house, even an apartment, and yes even if it is our home, if we plan on staying for more than a few minutes, we will clear the space. What does that mean? That means that we will enter, guns drawn and moving from one room to another to ensure that the space is clear of any other person. We do not do that in the homes of other vets, but we will explore the house so that we know what is in each room.

When Patti and I were house hunting, this little anxiety issue became a bit of a big issue. For her sake I never put a real estate agent up against the wall for appearing out of a side room to greet us. But for my sake, she started telling the agent to meet us out front and allow me to enter the building first and when I emerged then the agent could show us around. Still, for the first several years in our new home, I cleared it every time I stepped through the doors. Patti and the children made a game out of it. It was during the first cold Wisconsin winter that the building clearing needed to stop or at least allow everyone to enter the house and hang out in the kitchen until daddy was done. Finally, we got a dog that we left in the house while we were away. The dog met us at the front door with his tail wagging whenever we came home. That small act let me know that no one was in the house. That dog would not be wagging if there were someone else there. Patti wished that we had thought of that sooner.

Many vets, including myself, have issues with shopping. That sounds crazy right? Hear me out. We are okay with putting things in the cart, we are even okay with other shoppers as long as they do not crowd us. It is the funnel feeling when we go to check out that triggers us. We have a thing called the "fatal funnel" that we all learn to avoid like the plague. So, when we are pushing our carts toward the checkout stands, we are forced into a funnel shape and that triggers mass anxiety, and many times we act out. We get angry because we are afraid. We can no longer escape, so we are suddenly short-tempered and growling at our loved ones. We do not realize the issue until someone points it out to us, then comes the concerted effort to not feel this anxiety when forced into a funnel. For the sake of our loved ones, we work hard at stamping down that fear and that desire to push our way out of the situation. Sometimes, you will see a man or woman leave their cart and children in the checkout line. This is not a selfish gesture, this is a person trying to avoid the trigger, so they do not become mind-bending assholes for the remainder of the day.

Speaking of wanting to escape or run, most of us wear boots, even at home on the nice new carpet. We do that because we feel the need to always be ready to run. We cannot reach safety in flip-flops. Our feet need to be protected at all times because no one can run on damaged feet. So, we wear boots and even when we are sleeping our boots are placed neatly in the same spot every time, so we can find them in the dark and shove our feet into them. The same goes for our clothing. It needs to be in the same place every time we take it off. It sounds like obsessive compulsive disorder or OCD, and it is, and we cannot help it, but for the sake of our loved ones, we try. A few years ago, I graduated to strap on sandals in the summer. It was a monumental shift for us all.

Anyway, Dan; yes it is now time to talk about Dan. He had all of these issues and a few more. But he handled his anxieties in a very different way. Before he deployed for the very first time, Dan was a fun-loving kind of guy. He was the life of the party. When he returned, he was still a fun-loving guy and the life of the party, but he had almost no control over the words that came out of his mouth or the odd things that he did.

Let me give you an example: a group of people, men and women could be having a completely normal conversation about our assigned camouflage TDU's and somewhere in the conversation Dan would say something like, "Yeah, but they make your ass look funny'"or "They should put a flap in the back for all you Homo erectus people." Or something much worse. The conversation would inevitably go down a dark rabbit hole with sexual innuendo being thrown around like watermelon seeds at a picnic. The thread of the conversation would be lost amongst the laughing and general mayhem. This happened because Dan felt uncomfortable with so many people in the same room. So, he defused his fear by saying something outrageous.

These situations occur everywhere and anywhere for Dan, and no one is exempt from his release valve. Point in fact, early on after getting home, he was showering with his wife. She lathered her legs and bent over to shave her calf. That is when a thought occurred to him and instead of tamping it down as "not a good idea," he reveled in the thought of it and promptly peed on her back. It was the smell that tripped him up and as she was yelling, "Are you peeing on me?" she spun and punched him quite hard in the dick. He burst out laughing. Did she hurt him? Yes. But to him that pain was what he deserved. Oh, and she divorced him soon after. That little separation was good for both of them.

You see, Dan is one of those people who were taught by their denominational church that God says, "Thou Shalt Not Kill." But that is a misinterpretation, what the Bible actually reads is, "Thou Shalt Not Murder." There is a world of difference in those two words, "Kill" and "Murder." But Dan, like so many others, did not have knowledge of this distinction before they went out and killed for their country and their team or unit to stay alive. The Bible also tells numerous stories about men of God who, by order of God slaughtered entire cities right down to their animals and burned the food. Joshua comes to mind. But that is not taught by these denominations as a justification for killing, this is taught as a one-time deal and only if you have direct revelation from God Almighty can you kill anyone. Now David Berkowitz comes to mind.

It makes our job very confusing and folks like Dan, who has a really big heart and truly only wants the best for most people, end up blaming themselves for every single person that they had to kill. He came home believing that God could never forgive him for what he had done. He has since learned that it is Dan, who is not forgiving Dan. He also switched churches and is now learning a more accurate version of the Bible.

The point is combat vets all come home with some damage. How that damage is manifested is as diverse as the people. Some lash out and push people away to keep them out of danger, or just because they do not want to face the pain. Others get angry and become grade A assholes and again push people away and then there are those, and I have met only a few in my 25 years, that try to laugh everything away with inappropriate conversation, which also pushes people away. All of these defense mechanisms have one thing in common, they are trying to deal with their pain and guilt and the people around them need to understand that their loved ones are not trying to hurt them, it really is not about them at all. It is about the person in pain.

Dan was my spotter for about three years, but then he caught that Covid-19 crap, and the shit literally killed him. His wife kept him plugged in and after about a week, he woke up. Now his wife takes some credit for that miracle as she told God, "You don't get to kill him! If this son-of-a-bitch is going to die, it's going to be by my hand, so give him back. I'll kill him later." Of course, Dan has a different story that is much more "miracle" sounding, but I like his wife's version better. This is a different wife than the one he peed on, but he has done just as bad to his current wife. His new wife is more of a give-and-take kind of woman. He dishes it out and she dishes it right back or hits him with the spoon. Honestly, I don't think that he cares which reaction he gets, so long as he gets one.

Dan's shrink had quite the time with him. She had him do some of the same things that Doctor Cane did with me, but Dan was a lot more resistant. He really did not want to forgive himself. He was determined to keep his sin nature and all of the guilt that went with it. Can you tell that all these years in, I have finally found God and made my peace? I totally understand that scene in Forrest Gump where "Lieutenant Dan" is on the mast of the ship screaming at God and daring Him to strike him down. That was me, and it was my Dan as well. Some of us take longer than others and some, never make it through. Some of those are on the street living with their demons every day. And a lot of them die, having never felt another day of peace until the Lord called them home. Most of them were Korean War and Vietnam vets. The government never gave them shrinks. They just gave them drugs and sent them out into a country where the populace took out their anger and frustration on the men who had done their civic duty. They get help now, if they ask, but this help is a day late and a dollar short.

Anyway, Dan was my spotter for three years before he got sick. That Covid shit and the ventilator did a job on his throat. Now his vocal cords are fused together, and he cannot talk normal. He talks like Batman. So, he got a medical discharge and is now doing a consulting business from home. I am sure that he is driving his wife crazy, and she is loving every minute of it. That will be me soon.

———

The world feels like it has paused. The trees are sighing as the snow falls. And Mark and I are just part of the scenery. I love this silence. It allows me to just breathe... well as long as I do that breathing in an uneven cadence.

20

Murphy's Law

Let me tell you about my last deployment with Dan. I do not know if this happens to everyone, but it does happen enough that when I say Murphy's Law suddenly reared its ugly head, most people know what I mean. Murphy's Law means that shit is going to happen when you least expect it, or when everything seems to be coming up roses.

We were fine, me and the family. It was good. Then, I got deployed. This was not a normal deployment for me. This was a normal deployment for foot soldiers.

We got sent into the sandbox to hunt rag heads. Apparently, someone with more stripes than me thought that it was a good idea to push the bad guys out of a town that they were inhabiting. So, my number came up.

I packed like normal and was issued my Sadie, like normal, then, I got issued an ordinary rifle and a handgun. I did not ask any questions. But I figured that once we hit country, they were going to shelve my sniper rifle. This was going to be a rat hunt.

Do not get me wrong, they were always going to make me pack both rifles, but I would have scant use for Sadie.

So, we went to our pre-deployment training. That was where I got a lot more information and was okay with packing Sadie.

We hit country in the middle of the night and road in smelly old trucks across a wide expanse of sand until morning. About an hour after the sun rose, a town began to take shape on the horizon.

Soon the troops that we were joining came into view. They had been lobbing rockets and mortars onto the town for hours. The smell of gunpowder, sweat and piss were thick.

The plan was simple, we would go into the town on foot, that evening. Meanwhile, our allies would continue their barrage. There was no mention of the civilians who were most likely still inhabiting the town. It was a topic that simply was not discussed. I hate this kind of warfare.

Nighttime came too soon for me. I knew what we would find in the streets of that town, and I did not want to see it. At least it was night. Blood is not red in the dark.

We broke into squads. Normally, I would be a squad commander, but I was a sniper, a specialty unit, so I was in a specialty fire team with a Staff Sergeant Commander, who I had never worked with before. His name was Shane. He was a good man. Still is, as far as I know.

Each squad had two fire teams. Two of the squads had a specialty unit in the fire team, squad 1 and squad 4.

Our squad went to the far right. We stuck together as a squad until the specialty unit could find a place to stage an overwatch. Squad 1 did the same when they went far left.

Within a minute of entering the actual town, we were completely isolated. Other than by radio, we had no contact whatsoever with the other three squads.

There was some yelling and isolated gunfire far to our left. Then there was silence. We scampered down rubble-filled streets and ducked under dimly lit windows where the faint smell of food, and fear, and the crying of children and women escaped. There were no bad guys in there, just people trying to survive.

We stayed to the shadows. Occasionally, my silhouette was cast onto a mud brick building. In it, I could see Sadie's distinct shape sticking out above my head from her personal case, which was strapped to my back. I preferred to be behind her glass, looking at the enemy from a distance. Seeing her there, reminded me that, not only did I need to duck lower to get under things, but because I was not behind her glass, I truly needed to duck more. I was a trained shooter, not a scampering rat chaser. This was not my bailiwick.

As we traveled deeper into the town, the rubble became smaller in size. The debris here had not been caused by our allies and their mortars, this had been caused by gunfire and grenades. The chatter on the COMM's became fevered. Both fire teams for squad 2 were taking heavy fire. They were the second squad to the left. We were squad 4, and we were far to the right. We had entered in numerical order left to right, for the sake of simplicity.

A few seconds after squad 2 came under fire, both fire teams in squad 3 also came under heavy fire. Squad 1's specialty units were setting up their overwatch on a tall building. We had no such building, so, we scrambled forward and right as a squad.

It was a small town, but the mud and brick did a good job of absorbing a lot of the sound. It might have been the dimpling in the buildings caused by so much munitions damage. I do not know. All I know is that we were fine and then, we turned a corner, and we were not fine.

We, as a squad, were scattered across two streets. When we entered the town, it was decided that we did not want the two sniper teams in the same place at the same time just in case something happened before we could find a place to set up our overwatch. It was a good thing too because something happened.

When I say that "we" turned the corner, I mean that the first member of the part of our squad that I was with, turned the corner. The memory of the brilliant yellow-white flash that backlit his form will forever be burned into my skull. I was about two yards from him when he exploded in my face. The explosion threw me back and had it not been for my girl being strapped to my back, I might be paralyzed today. She saved my spine from wrapping around all the crap that was in the street. The impact knocked the air out of me and shattered Sadie's glass. I was still a great shot with iron sights, but it was nighttime, such shots would be a challenge. I registered the damage and the consequences of it in a split-second glance.

I rolled over and stuck my hand in something soft, squishy, and wet. I knew what it was, and most likely who it was. I did not need to look. It was not until Shane grabbed my shoulders and began yelling in my face, that I realized that, I could not hear him. I just shook my head. He understood and gave me some hand signals.

I was directed toward the roof of basically any house that faced the intersection. Dan headed for the first doorway, I wiped my hand on my blouse and followed.

The door had been blown off at some point. There was a great deal of debris on the floor and a dead child in the corner. We rounded a corner heading for the stairs up and found the corpse of the child's mother, probably anyway. It was hard to tell anything through our night-vision glasses. It was a woman, and I made an assumption. A man's arm was near her head. I could not see a body. We headed up the stairs.

There was part of a body on the stairs, it looked like it had been a young man. At the head of the stairs was a young woman, I will not describe what she looked like. We traveled down the upstairs hallway, clearing the doorways and rooms on each side as we went. My hearing began to return. I could hear the loud popping of gunfire, and another explosion that rocked the building and rained crap on our heads.

At the end of the hallway, next to an open window, the stairs to the roof appeared. We peeked out the window before ascending. I spotted a bad guy with a gun and shot him dead.

The stairs were clear of bodies. The top of the stairs simply emptied onto the roof. There was no cover. On the roof were four bad guys. We shot two before they even knew that we were there. The last two did not react quickly enough.

We pushed them aside and quickly set up Sadie. Without my hearing, using Dan as a spotter was stupid. He set up his M-16 and used his ordinary glass to shoot in a different direction than me. Between all of the over-watches, we managed to help make the ambush more of a fair fight. At least our men were no longer pinned down and helpless.

At first, we took a fair amount of fire from the overwatch of the bad guys, but in time we thinned them out and made some headway. I got my hearing back, at some point. I only know that we moved a couple of times before I could actually hear Dan yelling at me. There was far too much gunfire for anyone to actually talk. We had to yell.

As it turned out, the tall building that squad 1 had found, really had not helped us much. It was too far away to affect the fighting on the street. They ended up moving fairly early in the engagement.

But that's how you clear out the rats in a town, you play a game I like to call Russian roulette leapfrog. You dodge, and run, and shoot and yell, and dodge and fall, shoot some more, and sometimes you get out of it with only a few embedded chunks of building in your flesh, and sometimes, you go home in a body bag. It simply is not pleasant for anyone involved. You just do it and hope that you are lucky enough to tell the story later, or not, depending.

Anyway, our objective was to clean out the rats from this particular little town, and we did so to the best of our ability. I have no idea how many people we killed. I know that I expended all of my rounds, both for Sadie and for my M-16. I also know that nobody that I shot will be getting up again, but all of my rounds did not actually hit anyone. I ended up grabbing a rifle from the ground and using some of the enemy's rounds, which is not good. Their stuff is not up to specs. It tends to jam up our shit, because our shit is in specs, that's why you use their leftover rifles. I was not going to run that crap through Sadie. The M-16 might have been more tolerant, but I was not chancing it. It was a good thing that the battle was nearly over when I was reduced to local crap.

In the end, when we were pulling out, I was kind of glad that I had gone in with a crew that I did not know. So many of them would be returning in a bag. I am not saying that I did not acutely feel their deaths, I did, and I still do. I always will. But I was not as close to them. It sounds callous, right? God, I hope not. But it sounds callous to me. How could I not feel the same about these men, as I did about Chase, or Doug? Is it true that watching people die gets easier? How is that even possible? I do not know, and it is not true for me. Here I am, back at this question. It is a question for my shrink, and honestly, I do not think that she knows either. I think that those shrinks are mostly faking it, because all these years later, I still do not get it. I washed Corporal Michael Robert Gonzales off of my face and out of my hair, and yet, somehow, it all seemed so normal, ordinary, and expected and at the same time, I feel like I tried to shut my mind off and go somewhere else. I do not know. It was wrong, and there was nothing that I could do about it. Dan on the other hand, immersed himself and grew to like it. Then when he got home, he tried to just flip a switch and that did not work for him.

Corporal Gonzales did not have an open casket. But I helped put what was left of him in the ground all the same.

My shrink still wonders why I would rather be with my rifle and a spotter, instead of with a full unit. I have never had that problem. I never wonder. Sadie is better company, and other than that one mission, we seldom have the need to bring body bags for our friends.

Speaking of Sadie, she needed a lot of work when she came home from that shit show. I bent her barrel, probably when I fell on her, and cracked her stock, probably at the same time as the barrel and you know that I shattered her glass. That should give us all a hint on how many people I actually hit when using her to shoot. Still, I kept her upper and lower and replaced everything else. Funny thing, two deployments later, I had to replace her upper and lower and I got her another new glass and barrel. She needed a proper upgrade.

I tried to keep her up to speed. She was the reason that I can shoot so good. So, I kept her up to date, and I promised her that I would never land on her again. That was a harder promise to keep than I thought at the time. But, 25 years in the service generally throws a few curve balls at you.

And here I lie, in my 25th year, behind the glass of the girl that I named Mary, after the Blessed Mother. Sadie got retired to a life of ease several years ago. Mary is not a new model, well she is a new model, but not a new model of the same kind as Sadie. Mary is something new. She is a bonified beast, and I love her.

My latest shrink still has not wrapped her mind around Sadie, let alone Mary. I do not know what to tell her. A sniper and his rifle are a lot like a man and his car. It is something that you need to just accept, understanding is not required.

21

Life

All of this musing and remembering makes me want to sigh. Of course, I cannot do that. Not here. So, I smile. I have had a good life so far. It has been a bit rough, but I cannot become a diamond if I am not put under pressure. Patti said that to me once.

———

I remember it like it was yesterday. I had just returned from a successful deployment. "Successful" means that only the bad guys got to use the body bags. Anyway, I was in good spirits when I got off the plane and met her and the kids. I came into the base, not a civilian airport. There was no fanfare and no clapping, or worse, no civilians trying to pretend that they do not see the uniform, hoping that the military folks will just walk through and leave so that they do not have to pretend to be happy to see them. Most civilians are lemurs. They follow the trend of the day or even just the trend of the place that they are in. Right now, the military is now in fashion. Give it a decade or two and we will be back to being baby killers like our fathers who involuntarily fought in Vietnam. People are such hypocrites.

Patti, the kids, and I left the base for home. At home, I passed out some gifts that I had purchased while in the sandbox. For some reason, I had the urge when I was deployed to bring back some local flair. The kids were ecstatic. They ran off in almost no time to play with their new stuff. Patti and I were left alone to enjoy each other's company. It was a great homecoming gift, from them all.

I do not remember falling asleep. But I do remember waking up to the smell of a home-cooked meal. Fried chicken, mashed potatoes, and fresh green beans; there is nothing better. I got up, took a shower, and headed for the food.

Essentially, the first day was so normal that it would give anyone a good case of boredom. The next morning was something different.

Patti and I awoke to the sound of the blood-curdling scream of our daughter, Bella. We scrambled out of bed and bounced off of each other and the walls as we ran towards the screaming, which continued even after we had rounded the kitchen corner and found our daughter spilling blood all over the floor.

I grabbed the closest towel and closed on Bella. When I saw where the blood was coming from, I went blank, not immobile, just blank. I was no longer in my kitchen, I was somewhere else, and this child simply needed saving.

Somewhere in the kitchen, between the blood on the floor and the towel in my hand, I had put my handgun down to tend to my child. I had never just put the gun down before. My new shrink and Dr. Cane had made quite the fuss about that incident, not Bella, the gun, and putting it down.

Somehow, I learned how later, Bella had become impaled by a large drop-point butcher knife. It was stuck in her leg and was pointing out the other side. I quickly took the towel and crisscrossed the wound, holding the knife in place. Then, I scooped her up and headed for the door. Patti, meanwhile, had retrieved the keys, a couple of bathrobes, and our son.

I do not remember the drive to the hospital. I know that I was driving like a madman and the only thing that slowed me down was Patti's voice coming out of nowhere, "If you do not slow down, you could kill me and Michael." That comment cut through the fog.

The initial entry into the hospital was another blur. It was here that Patti took the lead. While I had been bandaging and driving, she had found out what had happened.

The children had been trying to get cereal for breakfast, allowing Patti and me to sleep in. Michael had encouraged his sister to climb onto the counter, after all, he did it all the time. All was well until, Bella had tripped, slipped or something. The next thing anyone knew, Bella and the butcher block were both tumbling toward the floor. The rest is history. I am still a bit confused as to how the bowls, which were what Bella was after and which were in a cupboard at one end of a fairly long counter, and the butcher block which was in the very far corner of the same counter, with a double sink in between, could have possibly intersected. Yet, somehow, they did.

The more important thing was the health of our daughter. It was impossible to be accusatory or angry with her health in question.

It was quite an operation for the doctors to extract the knife, and Bella was laid up for several weeks. In the end, the children both learned something, and Bella came out of it with a nice scar. Still, this type of thing is par for the course when you have children, and it was just the beginning of my week.

Bella stayed in the hospital for two days, for observation they said. She had hit nothing major, just her leg. They did not want her to strain anything, hence no walking and no fast movements. So, when we got a flat tire on the way home and the car jerked to the side, well that did not really count, right?

I have driven dozens of cars and had almost that many flat tires, but, having a flat on the front of a front-wheel drive, on a sketchy road surface, well now, that is a new experience.

Bella tensed up so much when the car jerked that she tore a stitch. The blood scared her, and she began to panic. Thank God for Patti and her seemingly endless patience. She dealt with the kids while I changed the flat.

The next day, I traded in the car for something a bit more stable and rear-wheel drive. We will not be doing that dance again.

Apparently, while I was at the car dealership, Patti was dealing with Jasper, our retired drug-sniffing service dog, who apparently thought that a skunk was a pound of coke. He brought the struggling creature into the house and presented it to Patti. He held it down while he patiently waited for the "Atta boy" and his treat for a job well done.

Poor Jasper, or poor Patti, I am not certain which one was more traumatized by that hapless skunk, maybe it was the skunk who was traumatized the most. According to Michael, it was absolutely the funniest thing that he had ever seen, watching mommy chase the dog, while the dog chased the skunk, while the skunk tried desperately to find a way out of the madhouse. Finally, without being prompted, Michael opened the front door and let the skunk run, while Patti tackled Jasper. Apparently, the two-hundred-pound of combined dog and human came to a skidding stop right in front of Michael, who giggled and pushed the door shut, then he said, "Mommy, you and Jasper stink."

Patti burned her clothing. The vet shaved Jasper, and they both bathed in some anti-skunk stink shampoo. Still, I could smell the skunk for days until I dragged the area rug and the couch, where Patti had been sitting at the time of the skunk incident, out into the yard and torched it all.

Michael and Bella both got a crash course on identifying the local wildlife. It was a tough sell for Michael to understand that the pretty black and white kitty was not a kitty, and it was the reason for the really bad smell.

It was after the smell was finally gone, i.e., after I had burned the rug and the couch and several other items, that Patti and I were chatting about the events of the week. Let's be honest, I was complaining about how ridiculous it had been when Patti reminded me that she had actually been the one who had calmed Bella and who had chased the skunk and tackled the dog. I guess I was not very conciliatory because Patti started to talk to me like I was a baby, and that is when she said, "Aww, poor baby, it has been a rough week for you, hasn't it? But, you know, all this pressure just makes you into a prettier diamond." Or something like that... no really, that was pretty close. So, you see how I interpreted her comment.

———

The thought of the skunk made me smile and want to scratch the beard that I had grown over the last couple of weeks. I did not of course. I just looked through the glass. There was a bit of a water drop on the bottom, but it would not hinder a shot.

The snow had stopped, and the wind had begun to tickle the world around us.

22

The last round to the first round

Bella was six when the knife incident happened, and yes, we all still tease her about it today, especially on Thanksgiving when we are carving the turkey, and no, it is not the same knife set, we gave that one away to charity and purchased a new one. Bella started kindergarten that fall. She still favored her right leg and if she ran a lot, she would begin to limp.

This fall, Bella starts college. She no longer favors her right leg or limps at all. She could have gone anywhere to get her bachelor's in criminal justice, the precursor for her law degree. She chose to attend Michigan State University; that's the Spartans, not the Wolverines.

Bella is not going to Michigan State just because Michael is going there, she decided as a child that she wanted to be a Spartan, not the Michigan mascot, an actual historical Spartan like in the movie 300. Michigan State was as close as she could get without time travel.

Oh, did I not mention that Bella is minoring in history? Sorry, that little bit of information definitely helps to fill out the story.

Like I said, Bella did not want any other college. She did not bother to apply, not that she actually needed to apply. Colleges were looking at her when she was in high school for her athletic ability in softball and gymnastics. Michigan State is not a huge recruiter for athletics, not like some of the other colleges, but, when they saw her application and then saw her athletic abilities, it was a done deal. They offered her a full-ride scholarship and she signed. Patti and I are both praying that it would be the match made in heaven that it appeared to be.

Michael is entering his sophomore year in college. He is on the rifle team and the swim team. Both are sports that allow for more individual achievement. Team sports are great, but Michael is a singularly gifted young man, much like both of his fathers, and needs to hog more of the spotlight. Patti would argue that this trait is also much like his fathers, I am not sure that I would agree, well Doug maybe, but certainly not me. I would not think of hogging the spotlight.

Michael was wined and dined by some of the biggest names in college sports. In the end, he wanted to stay close to home and he did not want to be at odds with his sister. That was strange for Patti and me. The children, as all children, have their sibling rivalries, but these two, they are close, not <u>Flowers in the Attic</u> close, but sibling close. Maybe it was the knife incident that truly activated Michael's natural protective instinct gene, maybe something else happened along the road of them growing up, I do not know. I do know that they are as close as siblings can be without living in each other's skin.

As a father, this makes me feel much more at ease with Bella leaving home to live in Lansing, Michigan. She will not really be living on her own, besides the fact that she will be living in a sorority, like Michael lives in his fraternity, she will have him close. That will almost be like I am there for her to lean on or hide behind or whatever.

I feel a tear welling up in my eye, again, this is becoming annoying. I blink it away and focus on the ground below my Mary. Mark shifts on his toe and his glasses come up. I adjust Mary. There it is, I see what Mark had heard. My ears must be getting weak.

Down the road, there is a small line of cars. The growl of their engines can be heard coming out of the sparse trees. It is echoing. If I had only sound to go on, I would not be able to pinpoint their location. Not for the first time, I thank the ancestors who built that road, for laying berms on either side of the road and making the road itself so very clear of anything that might hinder my shot. Thanks to them and their consideration, I have a clear line of sight of the road and anything on it for nearly 1200 yards. And 1200 yards is well within mine and Mary's range.

Mark's voice is soft in my ear. He is telling me that my target is in the first car. Well, that is unusual. Clearly, the bad guy has let his guard down a lot more than I had thought. "Feeling a bit cocky, are we asshole?" I think to myself.

Mark tells me the range and is updating the range as the cars move. He gives me wind mileage and direction. I adjust my glass to match. I have already chosen where the target will be on the road when I squeeze the trigger. He is getting close.

I see him in the back seat. This man is responsible for the deaths of over 10,000 people, and he is looking to double down.

He is a minor nobody, from a backward country that few people have ever heard of and those that have, know nothing about. Is it my right to simply eliminate him? I have never asked that question. I chose this life because I believe that what I do saves lives. If that means that I must carry this man's death on my conscience, then I gladly accept the responsibility. I know that somewhere in this country there are an entire population of people that would kiss my feet for what I am about to do. More importantly, they will be alive to kiss each other when they hear that he is dead.

More numbers come through the earpiece. I make a minor adjustment. I hold my breath, relax my body, and slowly breathe out, and squeeze. Mary barks. The sound of her voice is muffled by the suppressor, but the force of her voice throws snow into the air and shakes the leaves nearby.

Downrange, the rear window on the first car explodes, almost as if by magic. The man in the seat is shoved back against the cushion. The car itself rocks with the impact and the driver slams on the brakes in fear. The passenger cabin fills with red mist. All of this in mere seconds.

Meanwhile, the snow that had gathered on Mary's front site is bucked off, along with the snow that had accumulated elsewhere on her back. I reload and wait for confirmation.

Mark is silent in my ear for what seems like far too long, but then, like a dark angel he says, "Hit confirmed. Target down."

A long stretch of silence in my ear is punctuated by a mass of activity on the road. Men with rifles pour out of the trailing cars and begin to scan the world around them. They look straight at me. Can they see us? In the unlikely scenario where they see a chance glimpse of me or Mark, their rifles could never hit us, not without a marksman at the trigger. The rifles are capable of reaching this distance, but without a marksman, they would just be spraying lead in our general direction.

I am watching them. They are looking for us. The target is still unmoving. And then, before Mark confirms, I see my own kind of confirmation. The driver of the target's car opens the back door. A body spills out and the driver is shot on the spot. The target's body is pushed without gentleness or ceremony back inside of the compartment, and the armed guard lower their weapons and slowly return to their vehicles. One man takes the seat of the dead driver. They are in no hurry because there is no one in need of a hospital. The offending driver is left on the road.

"Confirmed. Let's get out of here." So, we do. But before I do anything else, I check my watch. I had hit my stopwatch when the cars first appeared, just to see how long Mark and I would wait for the target to be eliminated. A minute had passed. Just 58 seconds to be exact. One more minute in time, but for this soldier, it was a minute well spent and it was the last minute that I will spend behind Mary's scope looking for a human target.

The snow was coming down again. This time in huge wet flakes. The impressions that we were making in the existing snow would be gone in less than an hour. We had snowmobiles waiting a mile or so from our perch. It was an easy walk, my last walk. I took it leisurely.

Like the guards below, I was in no hurry. I had thrown my last round downrange on mission as a member of the United States Military. It was the last time that I would hear Mark whisper in my ear over an earpiece. Now it is his turn to talk or listen to someone else. I cannot help but smile as I put Mary away into her "house" as I call it and roll up my Gilly suit. We cannot linger, because they could have called in the hit, but I am not running either.

This, the last one, is a far cry from the one where I had lost so much. That time, I went home to bury my dead. This time, I am going home to my wife and children... to be alive. They are mine. All mine, and yet his as well. I am happy, and we are happy together in the home that we have built.

Now, Patti and I get to plan and build a restaurant that serves beer and wine with dinner, and maybe, just maybe, in honor of him, there will be a small bar attached where old snipers and military men and women from all branches, units, and departments can get together and raise a drink to our brothers and sisters who have gone ahead of us to whatever lies beyond. And the first round, every time, will be on me, in honor of them all.

ACKNOWLEDGMENTS

No author writes in a vacuum. They must get their inspiration from somewhere. This book is no exception, in fact, the inspiration for this book has come from many people. I would like to acknowledge those people who inspired the stories and events depicted on these pages. These people have shared their experiences, fears, and feelings and given me their immeasurable support in this project. In all of this, they have granted me a small glimpse into their lives, and I am eternally grateful for that sharing and caring. I would like to first acknowledge and thank, my sister Jean and my niece Laurie for their love and support and second, from my place of work I would like to acknowledge and thank the men and women who have made up the Air Force Military unit that I am honored to work with and especially those who directly encouraged me and contributed stories and information found on these pages, Retired Master Sergeant Danial Baldridge, Retired Chief Master Sergeant Michael DelSoldato, Senior Master Sergeant Todd Lawson, Senior Master Sergeant Paula Macomber, Retired Chief Master Sergeant Joe Martini, Retired Chief Master Sergeant Darren Pruden, Retired Senior Master Sergeant April Apo, Master Sergeant Kylea Sherman, Technical Sergeant Laremy Wonderley, Senior Airman Yazmeen Colin, Retired Army Sergeant First Class Gary Baker, and Retired Staff Sergeant Jimmy Ellison.

I would like, also to acknowledge my brothers, who all enlisted in the Military services, Stevie, Fred, Jim, Ed, and Neil. Some were more successful than others in Military life, but regardless, they have all touched my life and in doing so, contributed to this endeavor.

Finally, I will forever be grateful for my parents Steven and Marie whose stories will always find a way to be written on many pages and whose love, support and teaching gave me the courage to be who I am in all things.

ABOUT THE AUTHOR

Teresa Shafer, the child of multiple generations of American Combat Veterans dating back to the Revolutionary War, has finally written a book about a soldier. She has spent the last 20 years working with soldiers and learning what makes them do what they do and how what they do ultimately affects them and their families. When she is not working, Teresa enjoys a quiet life working in her yard and playing "where's the kitty" with her cat. She lives in an older community, in the shadow of a lovely Mountain, near the edge of a desert lake on the outskirts of Reno, Nevada.